Dark Earth
Rising

The Copper Man

Debra C

SHADOW
CANYON
— *press* —

ISBN: 979-8-9877469-2-9
Edited by: Lyndsey Smith, Horrorsmith Editing
Cover design by: James, GoOnWrite.com

*To my grandfather and great grandfather
who both labored in copper mines in Arizona.*

Table of Contents

Chapter 1

George Cunliffe teetered on the edge of the Lower Prestwich Bridge, his back to the yawning open-pit mine and everything that had made his life a misery.

What he did not feel was guilt. What he had done, he would do again.

He could not remember the drive to the mine, where he had left his truck with the evidence inside, or how he'd come to choose this spot to end his life.

Oblivious to the icy wind against his face, he stared down at the enormous tailings pond, the liquid a reddish orange on one side, running to a sickly yellowish green on the other.

The wind pushed the hood of his jacket from his head. Wooden floor beams of the old trestle bridge groaned beneath his feet.

Time to get going.

His hands were stiff but steady as he tested the strength of the vertical post closest to him and found it solid. After looping the old, frayed rope around the base of the iron shaft, he tied a knot, then slipped the noose around his neck. He'd intended to get right to it—leap into the air, arms spread wide, welcoming death—but he found he wanted to prolong his time on the bridge, just a little. Long enough to remember the one good, beautiful thing in his pathetic life that had brought him joy.

He picked up a small rock from the railbed and scratched words into the rusted track. When he was done, he tossed the rock into the tailings pond and admired his work.

I CURSE THIS PLACE.

Lowering himself onto the rail ties, he swung his legs over the side, one hand gripping a diagonal brace. He kicked off his boots and flicked the rope behind his neck, as if it were a scarf getting in his way. Then, before he could think about another thing, he pushed himself off.

A scream escaped his lips.

He hadn't meant to scream. The noise ended abruptly, and for one long moment, pain seared his neck as the rope tightened. His hands flew up to the noose, fingers clawing at the fibers, and then he was falling.

His body slammed into the pond's sludgy, sucking bank.

He lay there for how long?

Seconds? Minutes?

The rope had snapped, that much he understood. Even though death was not instantaneous, it was surely just a matter of minutes. His insides had to be smashed to bits. His mouth tasted like blood and metal. He stared up at the sky, the clouds turning a murky and sinister orange.

Or was the copper color of the water altering his vision?

Rain drops hit his face, sharp and distinct. By some miracle, he was still alive, standing. Floating above the tailings pond. He gazed down at his still body in wonder.

Transformed. That's what he was. His thoughts came in flashes. Images. Thinking in this strange new language.

His old life was over. His mind—the one that had been attached to his broken body—had carried over into this new, strange existence he'd yet to explore. It was like a warm yellow glow coming from under a door. He yearned to push it open and see what was there. Or *who* was there.

"Son?" he cried.

Instead, he heard the distant shouting of men and felt the wetness of rain falling upon his face. Then all was dark, except his mind.

Chapter 2

Hundreds of feet below the cliff where she stood, at the edge of a turnout, trucks the size of houses rumbled past.

The Prestwich Copper Mine was reopening.

After decades of avoiding the place, Leah Shaw had returned home to Tribulation Gulch, Wyoming. Minutes after crossing the county line, her thoughts had become increasingly morbid. She pictured her daughter lying facedown in a tailings pond.

Leah rubbed her eyes to dispel the horrible, unbidden image.

A glance over her shoulder confirmed six-year-old Harper napping in her booster chair in the backseat of the Blazer, soft brown hair falling over her face—safe. Leah turned her attention back to the scene below.

The open pit had remained just as she remembered. But now, the operation had moved underground. It had taken six years and millions of dollars to tunnel under the mountain of ore.

Soon enough, she'd get a firsthand look.

As a reporter assigned to cover the mine's controversial reopening.

Leah got back in the Blazer and drove toward the tunnel leading to Tribulation Gulch.

There was no avoiding the single-lane Prestwich Tunnel—so narrow the locals had nicknamed it the "Prestwich Squeeze"—unless she was willing to turn around, drive fifteen miles in the direction she'd just been, and come back up by an old state road.

"I have to pee," Harper said, now fully awake in the backseat. "And I want to see Gimme." Which was what her daughter had called her grandmother since she began speaking her first words at twelve months.

"Okay, sweetie," Leah said over her shoulder. "There aren't any potties until we get to grandma's house. Can you hold on for a little while?"

"I guess so," Harper said. Grudgingly.

Before Harper could start complaining, Leah began talking in a bright, overly enthusiastic voice that grated on her own ears. "Guess what we're about to do? We're going to drive through a really skinny and dark tunnel and—"

"I'm not afraid of the dark," Harper interrupted.

No. No, she wasn't. A fact which Leah found strange. Weren't children supposed to fear the dark? She'd even asked Harper's pediatrician about it. Did Harper lack imagination? Was there something wrong with her? Her brain? The doctor admitted it was "different" but not necessarily concerning. Harper had excellent verbal skills and exceeded most other milestones.

Leah glanced at her phone on the passenger seat. Four thirty. They would probably reach her mother's house around 4:45, if Harper's bladder held out.

A mountain covered in shrubs rose into the blue sky. Beneath it, the entrance to the tunnel loomed.

To the left of the arched opening was an old sign that read: THIS WAY TO TRIBULATION GULCH. Another on the right cautioned: NO PEDESTRIANS ALLOWED ON ROADWAY, with an arrow directing them to a walkway running the length of the tunnel. Five cars idled ahead of Leah, behind a thick red line painted on the road, waiting for the green light.

Leah took the opportunity to run her fingers through her hair, which she'd grown out since her divorce.

"Sexy revenge hair," her stylist had said. A mess, her mother would call it. Too busy to continue straightening it, she'd come to accept her natural waves, her hair falling about her shoulders in loose auburn curls.

Cars began streaming out of the tunnel, honking as they passed.

In the rearview mirror, Leah could see Harper frowning, straining against her seatbelt, leaning her head against the glass.

"Is our car going to fit?" Her daughter clutched the doll she'd named Chicken. Leah's ex-husband had bought it on a business trip to Estonia, and Harper had fallen in love with it. It had a human face, round staring eyes, pointed animal ears, and a beanbag body covered in gray flannel.

"We'll fit just fine," Leah said. "I've seen buses go through, but it's tight."

The stream of cars ended, and the light turned green. The narrowness of the tunnel made her swallow as they entered, the walls pressing in on both sides, and Leah's heart began to beat faster.

After a few moments, she relaxed slightly.

A long row of lights hung from the ceiling, but they weren't bright enough to banish the gloom. The elevated walkway with an iron pipe rail ran along the left side of the tunnel. Leah remembered racing along it in middle school, then back again, while a friend's older brother waited at the east entrance, smoking cigarettes in his truck.

Leah opened the window. An enormous fan kept the air circulating in the tunnel, but it still smelled damp and cloying.

"What's that sound, Mom?" Harper asked.

"It's water, sweetie. Tribulation Creek is nearby, and the runoff flows in a trench below that walkway over there."

A white Subaru directly ahead slammed on its brakes.

Leah gripped the steering wheel, muttering, "Come on, come on, let's go."

The car didn't budge.

When cars behind them began honking and Harper said, "What's happening, Mommy," Leah decided to get out and investigate.

She switched on the hazard lights. "I'm going to check on the people in that car," Leah said, turning off the engine. "You stay here, okay?"

Clutching Chicken, Harper nodded solemnly.

Leah ran ahead, approaching the vehicle warily, not sure what to expect. Maybe the driver was having a medical emergency. But the driver, a woman with blond hair swept up in a messy bun, alone in the car, was staring straight ahead, gripping the steering wheel. The woman startled violently when Leah tapped on the window. She heard the shriek through the glass.

"Are you okay?"

After a few moments, the window slid down. "I think I'm having a panic attack," the woman said, her voice hoarse, barely above a whisper. "I have claustrophobia. I didn't know I needed to take a tunnel."

The woman was young. Probably not even thirty, Leah guessed.

"There's an emergency turnout just ahead. Do you think you can drive there until the worst passes? There's a long line of cars behind us."

The woman shut her eyes and shook her head, clenching the steering wheel as if her hands were glued to it. "No, I can't. I don't know what to do. I'm freaking out."

Leah had experienced her fair share of panic attacks. Someone else would have to drive the car. In the woman's condition, she'd probably slam into the tunnel wall, and they'd all be screwed.

"It's going to be okay. What's your name?"

"Morgan."

"Okay, Morgan. I'm going to be right back. I'm alone with my kid, but I'm going to see if there's anyone who can drive your car out, and then you're coming with me."

Without waiting for a response, Leah ran back, giving a reassuring thumbs-up to Harper as she made for the first car behind them. The driver was alone. She kept going, ignoring his call asking for an explanation. Leah hurried toward a Jeep that had—thank God—a couple. Both wore hats that read: "The Ugly Bug Fly Shop."

Probably on their way to fish Tribulation River.

"I'm hoping you can help," Leah said through the open window.

The driver, a woman in her fifties with a tanned weathered face, nodded as Leah explained. "The poor thing. Tom can drive, can't you, Tom?"

Cars honked behind them.

Leah held up a placating hand. "We're on it," she shouted.

Tom was a big man with an enormous gut. He huffed beside Leah as they ran toward the Subaru. Morgan had the driver's side door open, legs out, head between her knees.

"Okay, Morgan, the sooner we get to my car, the sooner you're going to be out of here." Leah hauled the shaking woman to her feet and put an arm around her waist. At five-feet-eleven, Leah felt like an Amazon beside the petite woman with delicate features.

Tom jumped in the Subaru and drove off. Cheers went up from the line of cars. Leah helped Morgan into the passenger seat.

While she was buckling her up, like a child, Harper said, "What's wrong with the lady, Mommy?"

"She's feeling a little too sick to drive, sweetie." Leah slammed the door and ran around the Blazer.

"I'm Harper, and this is Chicken," her daughter said, thrusting her doll between the seats.

Beside her, Morgan's body jerked.

"Would you like to hold Chicken?" Harper said. "She makes me feel better when I'm sick."

Morgan shook her head, eyebrows lifting. "That's okay. But that's so nice of you to share your…doll."

The cabin suddenly smelled of sweat. The result of Morgan's panic attack, no doubt.

"Are you going into Tribulation Gulch?" Leah asked, hoping to distract the woman from her discomfort.

Morgan nodded. "Moving there. I got a job at the mine."

"Geologist?" Leah asked, curious.

"Nothing like that."

Leah thought it odd she didn't elaborate but decided not to press her. "Where are you coming from?"

"Utah. I worked at a coal mine and thought it was time for a change."

"Smart move." Leah peered in the rearview mirror at Harper, who was staring out the window, waving.

Leah followed her daughter's gaze. She was staring at the walkway. Leah expected to see someone there, a pedestrian, or a worker in a safety vest, but there was no one. A smile had come to Harper's lips, and her waving had become more enthusiastic.

"Whatcha doing back there?" Leah asked, mystified.

"I'm waving at the man."

Leah slowed and craned her neck for a better look. "I don't see anything, sweetie."

"Daddy says you need glasses," Harper replied, scowling. "Chicken can see him. Can't you, Chicken?"

Morgan was twisting around in her seat now. "Um, there's a shadow or something. That's weird."

Leah's fingers spasmed on the steering wheel. She wished she could stop the car, see what Morgan was talking about. But she couldn't. She had to keep driving.

"It's not a shadow," Harper said, voice rising. "It's a man. Why is he wearing that funny coat?"

Leah frowned into the rearview mirror. She had no idea what had gotten into Harper. Besides her attachment to Chicken and the adventure stories she made up involving her doll, her daughter was not prone to fits of wild imagination.

"She's freaking me out," Morgan muttered.

As they sped out of the tunnel and into the sunshine, Leah exhaled loudly.

"I can't see him anymore, Mommy," Harper announced.

At the first turnout, the white Subaru was waiting. Tom got out, a stubby hand holding the keys. "You okay to drive now?" he said to Morgan. "There's no reason to push it. I don't mind driving into town and meeting you there."

Morgan, hair disheveled, stared at the west entrance to the tunnel and the line of cars coming out of it. Her hands flew up to her mouth. "Please tell me that's not the only way back to the mine."

Leah sighed. "It is. Unless you want to drive an extra fifteen miles or so and go around the long way."

Morgan sagged against her car. "Fifteen miles? Are you serious?"

Leah nodded. She felt a stab of pity for the younger woman, who'd just discovered the tunnel of her nightmares stood between her and her new workplace. But that wasn't Leah's problem. She had to get Harper to her mother's house before her daughter's bladder exploded.

"I'm sorry, but I need to get going," Leah said. "Can you drive? Or would you like to take up Tom on his offer?"

Morgan bit her lip, and for a moment, Leah thought she might be stuck with Morgan for the next ten miles, but Morgan straightened and shook her head. "I'll be fine," she said.

Morgan got into her car, slammed the door, and sped down the highway, faster than the speed limit.

Tom's face turned red. "She didn't even say thank you."

"She's having a bad day," Leah replied. Though inwardly, she cursed the woman for her rudeness.

"That's generous of you." Tom gave her a little salute and waddled toward the Jeep.

Before Leah got back in her own vehicle, she stood surveying the mouth of the tunnel. All the cars had exited, and for once, there wasn't a line waiting to go inside. She could make out a bit of the pedestrian bridge, but the rest of it was swallowed up by the dark hole.

Something seemed to be moving, just behind a stretch of iron railing.

A shadowy figure.

She blinked, and then it was gone.

Debra Castaneda

Chapter 3

The front door flew open.

Harper threw her arms around her grandmother's knees, then shouted, "I have to pee!"

Patricia Shaw whisked Harper to the bathroom and returned to the formal dining room she used as an office. "It's so good to have you both here." She raised Leah's hand to her lips and gave it a quick peck.

"I really appreciate this, Mom," Leah said. And she meant it. Her mother had agreed to watch Harper while Leah reported on the reopening of the Prestwich Mine.

"I guess I have Jason to thank," Patricia replied, referring to Leah's ex-husband.

Leah snorted. "He can go screw himself."

In fact, he was probably screwing his new young wife at that very moment. Despite their messy divorce, Jason was an adoring father, but Leah didn't trust him in his besotted condition to properly look after their daughter. Especially after Harper mentioned he'd left her in the car while he dashed into the drycleaners. She'd lucked out with the timing of her assignment. Her mother was available and thrilled to spend time with her only granddaughter.

Leah avoided her mother's penetrating gaze and took in the many changes to the house since their last visit.

"The house looks great," she said. Built in 1910, it still had the original woodwork, doors, and light fixtures but had been converted from gas to electricity. When Leah lived in the house, the walls were covered in a hideous flocked wallpaper, but that had been ripped away, the walls painted a soft cream.

"I finally got the floors refinished and did a few other things I'd been putting off for years."

Leah walked down the hall to the bathroom. The door was so thick, it was impossible to hear anything. "You okay in there?" she called.

"I have to go to the other kind of bathroom now," Harper shouted. "I'm constipated."

Leah wondered where she'd learned that word. Probably from her new stepmother. She looked the type to have a weird diet.

Patricia's eyebrows shot up. "It looks like we have another over-sharer in the family."

Leah let that one go, mostly because she knew it irritated Patricia when she ignored her gibes. She leaned against the wall and stared down at her mother—five feet tall with a tight, compact frame. Large dark eyes. Brown hair with highlights to hide the gray. The two looked nothing alike. Not that she resembled her father either. He'd had a wiry build and black hair. His most distinctive feature was an exceptionally wide mouth with big, white teeth. "Chompers," he'd jokingly called them. Leah had been told countless times she looked like her great-grandmother, even down to her height. Her brother, Liam, on the other hand, had inherited Patricia's small frame and their father's wide mouth.

"So, you're going to keep the house?" Leah asked.

Patricia scowled. "Of course, I'm going to keep it. Where else would I go?"

"Closer to me and Harper?" Leah said mildly. Downsizing was a touchy subject for her mother.

"I may be seventy-two years old, Leah, but I'll remind you that I'm invested in this community. While my granddaughter is everything to me, I'm not ready to retire."

Patricia was a state lawmaker and an accountant with a busy practice. Leah had been lucky her reporting assignment coincided with the legislative break and the conclusion of tax season.

When Harper finally emerged from the bathroom, Patricia ruffled her hair. "How about I fix you some macaroni and cheese? I made salad for your mama and me, but you're not going to want that."

Leah didn't want a salad either, not after their long drive. She was starving. A chicken pot pie at the diner in town sounded good. And a glass of wine too—preferably tumbler-sized. Her mother didn't eat much and only stocked booze for special occasions. Visiting home was like going to a sober health spa.

After Leah had lugged the suitcases and Harper's bags of toys inside, they'd trooped upstairs, Harper spinning around in the wide hall.

"Your house is so big, Gimme," she cried. The wood floors creaked beneath her small feet.

"That it is, my dear." Patricia pushed the door open to the guest bedroom. "And this room is for my favorite granddaughter!"

Leah poked her head in. The double bed had a new coverlet in buttery yellow. The entire second floor had been painted a pretty, watery gray. "She could just sleep with me, Mom."

"No!" Harper cried. "You snore. And you said I could have my own room." She set Chicken down on the bed to stake her claim.

Her mother set Harper's small suitcase on a chair and frowned. "I thought you said you were going to talk to your doctor about that, Leah. Sleep apnea can be very dangerous. And you're too young to be snoring that loudly. Losing a few pounds might not be a bad idea either. Extra weight can cause snoring." The last bit was delivered in a singsong voice that made Leah grit her teeth.

"My mama isn't fat," Harper said. "She says she just has big bones."

Patricia blinked innocently. "I never said *that.*"

Leah shot her mother a warning look. Patricia didn't need to say it. She implied it, as she always had. Ever since Leah emerged from her gangly teenage phase with proportions some called "Amazonian," her mother had equated her height and musculature with being fat.

"Are you still running, dear?" her mother said.

Leah clenched her fists. "Five miles a day," she snapped. She'd run more if her busy schedule as a single, working mother allowed it.

The door to the room next to hers was closed. That was nothing unusual. Her mother kept it locked. Still, she couldn't resist. Her hand closed on the glass knob.

It opened.

She peeked inside and felt her insides drop.

Liam's bedroom was still intact. The single bed with the blue coverlet decorated with horseshoes. The wood-framed cowboy posters. A wagon wheel hanging on the wall above a headboard made from an old fence.

Liam had been dead for thirty-five years.

In all other respects, her mother was fine. More than fine. Besides her work as a legislator and accountant, she'd championed the new Prestwich Mine. But when it came to Liam's old bedroom, it was downright creepy. Instead of packing it all up, as she'd promised last Christmas, her mother had the floors refinished and two of the walls painted a jaunty red. Then she'd put everything back.

What the fuck?

Harper pushed past her. "Is this *your* room, Mom?" she shouted. "I want to sleep here. I want to sleep here!"

Leah's mother appeared, eyes wide, face white. "No," she said. "No, she can't."

"But I love it!" On tiptoes, Harper whirled around to face her mother. "I didn't know you liked cowboys, Mom!"

Leah pressed a hand to her forehead. There was no easy way out of this, other than the truth. Her mother was staring at Harper, aghast, her mouth opening and closing like a fish.

There was nothing to do but tell her. She'd find out anyway, eventually. The Copper Man was a local legend. Leah could imagine how it would happen. Harper would be invited to a playdate, and the moment the children were alone, some kid would ask Harper about her uncle.

Leah crossed the room, swept Harper into her arms, and sat on the bed, pulling her daughter onto her lap. She gave her mother a look that said, *Let me handle this.*

Harper reached up and stroked the side of her face. Leah kissed her daughter's fingers, then cupped her chin.

"Harper, you're a big girl, so I'm going to tell you something. You were too little before."

Harper had recently turned six, and she nodded. "I'm going into the first grade." In Harper's mind, kindergarten was already synonymous with "little."

"Yes. I'm going to tell you about something bad that happened when *I* was in kindergarten, but I don't want you to be too sad because it happened a long time ago."

Leah glanced up in time to see her mother's face collapse. Then a moment later, she was gone.

Leah took a deep breath and continued. "I used to have a brother. This was *his* bedroom. His name was Liam."

Harper's eyes snapped open. Before she could interrupt, Leah held up a hand.

"But Liam died when he was five and a half years old."

Harper slid off her lap and stared at her with serious dark eyes. "You never told me."

Leah shook her head. "No. You were too little, and I was afraid I'd make you too sad."

"I didn't know him," Harper said, frowning.

"No. But I wish you had. He was very nice." A sob rose in her throat, and she choked it down. "If he'd lived to grow up, he would have been the best uncle ever."

"Did he have cancer?" Harper asked. One of her kindergarten classmates had died of a brain tumor.

Leah shook her head. The next part was going to be tricky. She had to provide enough information, in a matter-of-fact way, without frightening her daughter. "No, nothing like that. He wasn't sick." She paused. "One day, he was out playing, and a bad man took him. He hurt Liam very badly, and he died."

Harper blinked rapidly. "I'm not allowed to play outside by myself," she said, a slight warble to her voice.

Leah's heart twisted in her chest. Not much scared Harper, but her daughter sounded unnerved. Not that Leah blamed her.

"Things were different when I was a little girl," she said hurriedly. "This is a small town, and we were allowed to run around more than kids today." An exaggeration. Her mother always wanted to know where they were going, and with whom, and they had to be home by a certain time. But things had taken an unexpected turn that day in July. Leah cleared her throat. "The man was very bad. He'd taken other kids too. Then one day, he took Liam."

Harper sniffed. "Is the bad man in jail?"

"No, sweetie. He died. And nothing bad has happened around here in a very long time, so there's no need for you to be worried."

Harper looked past her, at the row of cowboy posters. "Did he hurt any little girls like me?"

Her daughter's hair had come unclipped, and it tumbled over her face. Leah tucked it behind her ear. Her hair was fine, like her father's, and glossy.

"He did," she said in a quiet voice.

Harper might not have been afraid of the dark, but it was obvious the story had disturbed her. She was fidgeting, and her little heart-shaped face was pinched with worry. It was time to drop the subject.

"Would you like to see some pictures of Liam?" Leah asked.

Instead of answering, Harper looked around the room. The closet was wide open, empty except for an old broken lamp on the floor. Patricia had finally managed to clean out the clothes that had hung there for years—moth-eaten and disintegrating. Harper's eyes eventually landed on the wooden trunk at the foot of the bed, decorated in faded cowboy motif stencils.

"What's in that box, Mom?"

"Liam's old toys."

"I want to play with them," Harper said, in a tone that anticipated opposition.

Leah tweaked her nose. "We have to ask Gimme first." It was hard to imagine her mother refusing her own granddaughter something like that, but when it came to Liam's things, her mother was extraordinarily protective.

Harper glanced at the chest, then scowled at her mother, all talk of a killer seemingly forgotten. "Liam would want me to play with his toys," she said, voice rising. "You said he would be a *nice* uncle." Before Leah could stop her, Harper was pounding out of the room, shouting, "*Gi-mme!*" at the top of her lungs.

Chapter 4

After Harper was tucked in bed upstairs with a firm warning to stay there, Leah's conversation with her mother went as she'd expected.

"I don't want her playing with Liam's old toys," Patricia said as they cleaned the kitchen. "That would be too hard for me. Seeing his things around like that, after all these years. And besides, those toys are so old. They're probably covered in lead paint." She grabbed a dishcloth and began wiping down the counters. "I'll tell you what. I'll take Harper to the Mercantile later today, and she can pick out whatever she wants. She'll forget all about those old things."

Leah sighed. "This is Harper we're talking about." Since spotting the toy chest in Liam's room, Harper had talked of nothing else.

"As much as I adore that child, Harper needs to learn no is no." Her mother hung the dish cloth on a hook. "In fact, I would prefer if Harper didn't go into his room at all. I'll call the locksmith tomorrow."

"Why's the lock broken?"

"One of the painters must have manhandled it," her mother said, looking up at the ceiling and frowning.

Leah followed her gaze. She could hear it now too—the creaking of floorboards. Harper was on the move.

"Is she still wandering around at night?" Patricia asked sharply.

Leah scraped a hand through her hair. The texture felt off. Stringy and clumpy. She needed a shower as much as she needed a drink. And she was still hungry after her paltry dinner. The salad had chicken in it but not enough to satisfy.

"Yes, she still gets up," Leah admitted. "But not as much as she used to."

"Any wandering at night when the adults are asleep is too much in my book. It's just not safe. What if she went outside? Can't you lock her in?"

A vein in Leah's forehead began to throb. She rubbed it as she unclenched her jaw. "No, Mom, I will not lock her in. What if there was a fire? If I did something as extreme as that, Harper would tell her teacher, and the next thing you know, I'd have social services at my door." Leah wagged a finger at her mother. "And don't you do it either if I'm not around."

Her mother's eyebrows shot up. "Oh? Do you have plans to go gallivanting around and having sleepovers?"

Leah snorted. "Hardly. Tribulation Gulch isn't exactly Club Med for singles."

Her mother studied her through narrowed eyes. "You haven't heard, then?"

"I have no idea what you're talking about."

"You'll see," her mother said in a singsong voice. A floorboard groaned over their heads. Patricia scurried out of the kitchen, and Leah could hear her calling up the stairs. "I'm coming up now, Harper, and I better find you in bed, young lady."

Small feet pounded, followed by the slam of a door.

Leah stood at the bottom landing, one hand gripping the round cap of the newel post, staring after her mother. "Mom. What did you mean? I'll see about what? You can't just leave me hanging like that."

Her mother stopped on the top landing, a slight smile on her lips. "Watch me."

After her morning run, Leah jogged into town with the aim of finding something heartier to eat than fat free yogurt and blueberries. For Harper, there had been pancakes, but when Patricia said, "Oh, you don't want these, do you? So many carbs," Leah made her excuses. Something about checking out the new businesses downtown for an article she had to write, which was mostly true. But first, food.

Her mother and Harper hardly noticed her departure. That's the way it usually was when the two were together, wrapped up in each other's company.

The outside air was a chilly forty degrees. Leah jogged the half mile to Center Street, the hub of Tribulation Gulch, population two thousand. She passed a mix of large, well-tended Victorian homes and rundown properties with yards choked with weeds and porches cluttered with junk. The closure of the old Prestwich Mine in 1989 had hit the town hard, but there were signs of better times ahead. She counted half a dozen SOLD signs. A good number of houses were undergoing major remodeling.

From the center of town, Leah took in the spellbinding view of the towering Absaroka range.

Tribulation Gulch was fiercely proud of its rustic, Old West appearance. The town had log buildings, including the post office and three saloons, and raised boardwalks instead of sidewalks. The Greek Coffee Shop, the Starlight Diner, and Dobb's Grocery were still there with their Western false fronts, as was Bart's Mercantile and the barbershop.

Leah slowed to a fast walk and passed a three-story hotel, a bed and breakfast, and a fishing tackle shop called Hook 'Em. Those were new.

The far end of the street was unchanged: Tribulation Elementary, a series of nondescript duplexes, and two-story apartment buildings in blond brick. Around the corner were the combination junior and senior high school, the new City Hall, and the old one—a wooden shack built in 1884 with a plaque testifying to its historic significance.

Stomach rumbling, she entered the Greek Coffee Shop. For once, she didn't recognize anyone. Most of the customers appeared to be tourists dressed for hiking and fishing. She sat at the counter, where she was waited on by a young woman with long black hair and hooded eyelids painted metallic gray.

"I'll start with coffee, please. By any chance, are you Eleni's granddaughter?" Leah asked, trying not to stare at the elaborate skull tattoo on the girl's chest. It must have hurt like hell.

"You guessed right," she said. "I'm Zoe. From Salt Lake. It's my turn to help the grandparents this summer. New in town?"

"Nope. Back home for a visit."

Zoe slid a menu across the counter. "Oh yeah? Who's your people?"

Leah studied her for a moment. Early twenties, maybe. Her breathy voice an odd contrast to her edgy look. "I'm Leah Shaw. My mom is Patricia Shaw." She waited for the usual reaction.

"You're kidding? I never would have guessed. You don't look anything like her."

Leah nodded but said nothing. She needed coffee, but she didn't want the girl dropping the pot when she figured it out. A slight frown had come to Zoe's face, head slightly tilted. She was almost there.

Zoe's eyes bulged. "You're that lady. The one with the…"

Murdered brother. That was her, all right.

Leah looked away, biting her lip. When she finished counting to five, she said, "I could really use some coffee and something to eat."

Zoe turned red under her pale shade of foundation. "Oh, I'm so sorry. Of course. Regular coffee, or a latte or something?"

Looking past her, Leah spotted an enormous, shiny espresso machine on the counter. That was new since her last visit, along with the modern window blinds that had replaced the ancient floral cafe curtains.

"I'll take a latte with a double shot," she said.

For breakfast, Leah skipped the bacon and sausage—even though her mouth watered at the savory aroma wafting from the kitchen—and ordered a Greek omelet, opting for greens and wheat toast instead of the fried potatoes on the side.

With tables turning over, Zoe was kept busy, so there was no time for further conversation. Leah pulled out her phone, connected to the WiFi, and caught up on the news while she ate. The feta cheese was incredible, but then again, it always had been. It was made by a local called "The Goat Man." She'd occasionally seen him tending to his herd of goats as she ran through the hills above town years ago.

Leah pushed back her empty plate, paid the bill, and headed straight to the bait and tackle shop, Hook 'Em, which was already doing a bustling business. She stepped inside, the bell on the door jingling. The owner, Colt Carter, was more than happy to talk to her when she introduced herself as a reporter with a national news site. So thrilled, he didn't seem to notice she was wearing jogging pants and running shoes.

She sat in a camp chair, looking around as the owner answered a customer's questions about guided fishing trips. The middle of the shop was devoted to a massive selection of flies in wooden bins. Reels and rods were displayed on the walls, along with vests and waders.

When Colt finally wrapped up with the chatty customer, he strode across the shop to where she was sitting next to a hat rack. "I'd invite you into the office, but it's a mess back there."

"We're fine here," she said.

Colt was of medium height with a shaved head and black beard, and behind black-framed glasses, his dark eyes were large and serious. He explained he moved from Arizona after discovering Tribulation River and deciding the area was perfect for his business.

She held up her cell phone. "Do you mind if I record our conversation?"

"Not at all," he said, smiling. "If that means I won't be misquoted, then it's fine by me."

Leah pressed record and set the cell phone on a shelf. "So, you didn't know about the mine reopening until *after* you decided to come here?"

Colt gave a sheepish shrug. "I'm pretty sure someone mentioned it, but I guess I wasn't paying much attention. The truth is, even if I *had* known about it, it wouldn't have stopped me. Not after I fished Tribulation River."

"The river has that effect on people."

Colt nodded, looking pleased she understood. "Exactly. It's surprising somebody else didn't see the opportunity. Ever since we opened, we've been selling out our guided fishing trips. When I finally understood that mine was starting up again, I was shocked. I was sure the deal would fall through. Someone, somewhere, had to have some common sense and put a stop to it. But the people around here? They act like it's the most wonderful thing in the world, to have a copper mine practically in their backyards. It's fucking insane, excuse my language. You know how many people have wells around here? Most everybody. If something happens to that tailings pond dam, all that shit is going straight into the creek, and then into Tribulation River. And guess what? There's no coming back from that. Ever. The river would be fucked. As in, permanently."

Colt glared at her as if she was personally responsible for the disaster he'd just predicted. When he noticed her expression, he exhaled loudly.

"Sorry. My wife hates it when I get started like this." He shook his head. "But man, this whole thing has me worried, you know?"

Leah *did* know. Exactly. Mining was, and continued to be, a high-risk operation, for the workers *and* the environment.

Colt looked her over with a hopeful smile. "Are you coming tomorrow night?"

"I'm taking a media tour of the mine during the day tomorrow, but nothing tomorrow night. What's happening?"

Leah ended the recording on her phone and slipped it into her jacket pocket.

"A meeting about the mine reopening. There's a sign outside the shop. I thought that's why you'd come in." He pointed at a poster tacked up on a corkboard covered in flyers. It read: LET'S HOLD PRESTWICH TO ITS PROMISES.

Leah walked over for a closer look. The agenda was included, in easy-to-digest bullet points: *Prestwich Tunnel Construction. Old tailings pond. Worker housing. The company has yet to provide detailed plans!*

Leah turned to Colt in surprise. "Isn't it a little too late for something like this? The grand opening is the day after tomorrow."

"Not at all," Colt answered, pushing up the sleeves of his sweatshirt. "We need to keep up the pressure. The company made a bunch of promises, but it hasn't given us a plan, or a timeline. They've always got some excuse, and we're still waiting."

"Is anyone from the company coming?"

"Supposed to. They always send some public relations flack, but we'll just have to see."

Leah turned to leave, then stopped. "Thank you. I'll be there." Tomorrow would be a long day, starting with a tour of the mine, then some writing time, followed by an appearance on a cable news show, and now, a town meeting.

Colt shoved his hands into the pockets of his fleece vest and rocked back on his heels. "When you go on that tour, see if you can get anyone to talk to you about the workers getting spooked and the accidents they're trying to keep under wraps."

"Accidents?" she repeated. It was the first she'd heard about that.

The door opened, letting in a blast of cold morning air. A group of half a dozen men trooped in.

Dropping his voice, Colt said, "So I keep hearing. Nothing too serious. So far."

Chapter 5

The next morning, after pouring herself a mug of coffee in the kitchen, Leah poked her head into the living room, where Harper was busily arranging tiny figurines on the coffee table. Patricia sat in an easy chair, dressed for the day in jeans and a navy pullover, reading a book. A biography of Margaret Thatcher. It was an elegant but comfortable room, with large windows overlooking the front yard.

"You better get a move on if you don't want to be late," her mother said.

Wearing a camisole and the old sweats she'd slept in, Leah leaned against the archway, watching her daughter place fairies inside a circle of red mushrooms. The box on the floor next to Harper appeared to hold at least fifty pieces. Harper was so engrossed in her project, she didn't seem to register her mother's arrival.

"The tour doesn't start until ten," Leah said. "It got pushed back at the last minute." She padded over to Harper and kissed the top of her head. "That looks fun."

"It's a magical kingdom." Harper held up a tiny gnome for inspection.

It was no box of cheap toys. They were beautifully crafted and painted. Leah wondered what it had cost but decided not to ask. If her mother wanted to splurge on her granddaughter, Leah was more than happy to let her.

Chicken sat atop a pink castle, presiding over the kingdom with round, dark eyes.

Leah kissed her mother on the cheek and was instantly enveloped in aggressively floral perfume.

Her mother looked up, surprised. "What was that for?"

"For that," Leah said, nodding at the new toys. "She loves them."

"And I love that child." Getting to her feet, Patricia added, "Come on, Harper. Why don't we take a break and get some breakfast?"

Harper shook her head. "I can't, Gimme. I have a lot to do here."

Patricia threw her head back and laughed. "Where does this child come up with this stuff? Okay, Harper, you win. You stay here, and Gimme will bring you your breakfast, and you can eat in here, okay?"

"That works for me," Harper said, making Patricia laugh again.

Upstairs in the bathroom, Leah set her robe and clean underwear on top of the hamper, then turned on the tap. The ancient pipes rumbled in the wall. When the water was hot enough, she stepped inside the claw foot tub and washed her hair with the fancy shampoo her mother used. A floral, musky fragrance filled the room, and she breathed it in, smiling. It smelled amazing. She let the conditioner sit in her hair while she shaved her legs for the first time in weeks. When she was done, she flipped her head over and turned off the hot water, letting the cold water hit her hair, a trick she'd learned to keep her wavy hair from frizzing.

Leah was reaching for the handle when she noticed the water turn reddish-orange, and she jumped back. The stream had thickened too—more like milk and just as opaque.

It had to be the pipes, rust discoloring the water.

She dried off, wrapped a towel around her head, and hurried downstairs. "Are you having trouble with the water down here?"

The kitchen was awash in soft morning light. Her mother was at the sink, filling an electric tea kettle. The water was running clear. Her eyes widened. "No. What happened?"

When Leah finished explaining, her mother sucked in her breath, then exhaled loudly.

"It's got to be those darn pipes. My plumber has been after me to replace them, but that's another thing I've been putting…" She set the kettle down on the counter and raised one hand in the air, frowning. "Did you hear that?"

Leah froze.

From down the hall, Harper screamed.

Leah's heart jackhammered in her chest. She thundered down the hall, her mother close on her heels. She yanked on the bathroom door, but it was locked from the inside.

"Harper?" she shouted, pounding on the door.

"There's blood in the toilet, Mom," Harper said. "It's gross."

Leah's legs wobbled with relief. "It's okay, Harper. I think I know what it is, but you need to open the door so I can check."

A moment later, the door opened, and Harper stood there in her purple pajamas, lips curled in disgust. She pointed at the toilet. "It's red," she said, then stomped past Leah and threw her arms around her grandmother's waist.

Leah peered into the porcelain bowl. Sure enough, it was filled with the same reddish-brown color that had startled her during her shower. Which made sense. The bathroom on the first floor was directly beneath the bathroom on the second floor, so they shared the same pipes.

"I think it's just rust, sweetie," Leah explained. "From the pipes." But as she stared into the toilet, she wasn't so sure. Rust-tinged water wouldn't have a thicker consistency, would it? She was positive it wasn't blood. As a woman, she considered herself an expert on the subject.

Her mother reached around her and flushed the toilet. "Yuck," Patricia said, then she looked around, hands on hips, nose wrinkled. "Do you smell that?"

Leah took a cautious sniff. A faint odor permeated the room—something musty and slightly acrid. "It's probably coming from the rusty water."

Her mother went to the window and flung it open. Cold mountain air rushed in. Another brisk morning in Tribulation Gulch. The bathroom tiles chilly against her bare feet, Leah stepped into the warmth of the hall, wishing her robe was heavier.

Harper returned to playing in the living room, the toilet incident seemingly forgotten.

The brief scare had left the two women breathless. They watched Harper, their bodies nearly touching. Patricia stepped closer to the coffee table and pointed. "What's that?"

Something shimmered in the middle of the fairy circle.

"Is that a copper nugget?" Leah asked, leaning over the table.

It was. Of course, it was. She'd seen hundreds of them over the years. Smelted and slightly polished, they were sold all over town as souvenirs. The question was, how had Harper gotten ahold of it? After a detective had told her parents a copper nugget had been found in a pocket of the jeans Liam was wearing at the time of his death, Patricia had turned the house upside down, searching for copper nuggets, and had thrown them all away, including the collection Leah had kept on her bedroom dresser.

It was how The Copper Man had come by his name.

A nugget left with each of his victims.

Leah looked at her mother. All color had left her face. She rubbed her chest as if it hurt.

There had to be a perfectly reasonable explanation. The nugget had come from somewhere—probably the store where her mother had bought the toys.

Leah crouched next to Harper, plucked up the nugget, and held it in front of her daughter. "Harper," she said, "this is pretty. Did it come with the toys?"

Harper, who was too busy building her fantasy fairy world to notice her grandmother's alarm, shook her head. "No. It was just there."

Patricia coughed behind Leah.

"I don't understand. You must have put it there, sweetie. Didn't you?" The words, even to Leah's own ears, had the faint ring of an accusation.

Harper sucked her cheeks in. "No, I didn't," she said, voice rising. "It was just there. When I got back from going to the bathroom."

Leah straightened. "Liam used to collect them," she said to her mother. "Did you ever look through his toys?"

Patricia shook her head. "No. No, I never opened the toy box after…" She closed her eyes. "I couldn't."

Leah tipped her head in Harper's direction. Patricia's eyes snapped open in a flash of understanding.

Before her mother could scold Harper, Leah said, "Sweetie, did you go into Uncle Liam's room? To see what was in his toy box?"

Harper jumped up, face flushing. "No. I didn't. You told me not to." Her eyes slid to the floor, and she swallowed. "I did go into his room, though. I heard something in there, like someone was talking, but there wasn't. I wanted to open the toy chest, but I didn't." She crossed her heart with a little finger. "I pinky swear."

Leah studied Harper. The firm set of her jaw that ended in an adorable chin quivered slightly.

"When was this?" she asked her daughter.

Harper shrugged. "I don't know. Last night, when you and Gimme were sleeping. No one was in there, and I turned the lights on and everything. But the toy chest was open, so I closed it. I didn't want you to think I did it and get mad at me." Harper took the copper nugget from her fingers and studied it for a moment. "What is it, Mom? Why does Gimme look sad?"

Patricia sat in a chair, staring down at her hands.

Leah rubbed the side of her face, thinking. Harper had heard enough of Liam's disturbing story. Leah didn't want to make it more complicated by explaining why the copper nugget had distressed her grandmother. And while Harper denied taking anything from Liam's toy chest, it was the most obvious explanation. Harper rarely lied, but she might if she thought she'd done something to upset her Gimme.

"What is that thing, Mom?" Harper repeated, tugging on the belt ends of her robe.

Leah slipped the nugget into a pocket and combed her fingers through her hair. It was still wet. She needed to get ready, or she'd be late for the mine tour. "It's a bit of copper. You remember when I told you all about copper, right, and how the miners get it out of the earth?"

Harper nodded solemnly. "Yes. My grandpa was a miner."

"Sort of," Leah said. It wasn't worth explaining Harper's grandfather had worked as a lead project engineer for the company. She turned to Patricia, who was busying herself with plumping up the sofa cushions. "Are you going to be okay, Mom?"

Her mother flapped a hand at her. "Of course, I am. It's just, you know, it'll be his anniversary next month, and I always get a little…" Her voice drifted off.

An old, familiar heaviness settled into Leah's stomach as she climbed the stairs. The anniversary of Liam's death was less than a month away. The Fourth of July. A holiday she'd come to dread.

.

Chapter 6

The yawning open-pit mine was hidden behind a series of Quonset huts. Leah didn't think it was any mistake the giant gash in the earth had been obscured from view. It was hideous—an ugly open wound spoiling the ruggedly beautiful western Wyoming landscape. At least the hole wouldn't get any bigger. The new operation had stopped destroying the land and instead moved below ground, with tunnels stretching under the earth.

Leah stood shivering in the cold morning air as the small group of reporters waited for the arrival of the communications director. Not many journalists had shown up for the mine tour: a young woman with a round face and glasses from a wire service; two middle-aged men from Salt Lake City, representing a newspaper and the public radio station; and a TV news crew from a conservative cable news network.

The TV reporter, recognizing Leah from her appearances as an environmental expert on a competing cable network, introduced himself as Randall King. He had a fleshy face and obviously dyed caramel-colored hair.

"You going down into the mine?" he asked.

For the first time, Leah took in his attire. He wore jeans, a brown corduroy jacket over a polo shirt, and hiking boots.

"Are you?" she asked, unable to keep the suspicion out of her voice. "I was told they weren't letting reporters in."

"We're going," Randall said. "Someone at the assignment desk set everything up. We're acting as pool."

The photographer, holding a video camera, leaned toward them. He was so young—he couldn't have been more than a few years out of college.

"Hi, I'm Daniel." He offered his free hand. "Don't worry. We won't jerk you around. I'll upload the pool video as soon as we get back to the satellite truck."

There was no way in hell she was going to rely solely on pool video. Watching video shot by someone else wasn't the same as seeing the mine with her own eyes. She needed to see the operation for herself, and she was furious her request to see the underground operation had been denied. "The tour will be above-ground only," an email said. Either the mine officials had lied, or the news network had pushed back and convinced the PR flack to let them shoot pool video for everyone else.

Leah felt her face twisting with irritation. She forced a smile to her lips. It wasn't Randall King's fault she'd been cut out. "Thank you," she said. The words came out more stiffly than she intended.

Leah turned to two towering A-frame structures and a giant metal circle that reminded her of a Ferris wheel. All the buildings were painted a warm sand color. The Absaroka Mountain Range wasn't visible from where she stood, but hills fondly dubbed "The Dinky Minors" rose into the cloudless blue sky beyond the mining operation and the old tailings pond. She could just make out the top of the rail trestle that

once ferried cars full of ore over the toxic pond—also the spot
The Copper Man had chosen to end his life.

Leah, standing apart from the other reporters, watched
workers in hardhats and neon vests unload boxes onto palettes
from the back of a semi-truck. They ignored the group of
reporters. Leah suspected the new PR flack had warned the
employees not to talk to them.

"Hello! Hello! Sorry I'm late."

Leah spun around. A petite woman with blond hair was
striding toward them. It was the woman who'd had the panic
attack in the Prestwich Squeeze.

So, Morgan *was* the new head of communications. She was
casually but stylishly dressed in skinny black pants, a striped
top, and a fawn jacket. Her pointy ankle boots matched the
color of her jacket. Very pulled together, compared to the
rumpled disaster she'd been the day before.

Morgan stopped and stared at Leah, cheeks flushing. She
raised a hand in greeting, but it was obvious from the tight set
of her jaw, she was unhappy to discover her rescuer was a
reporter. The young woman was doing her best to hide her
embarrassment. She clapped her hands and said in an overly
loud voice, "Thanks for coming, everyone! So glad you can be
here."

Leah followed the others as Morgan led them to a
Quonset hut, talking all the way. The TV news photographer
began shooting. Inside, Morgan led them to a nondescript
room with hard chairs, where they watched a video explaining
the transition from an open-pit mine to the new block caving
method. Even though Leah was familiar with the process, she
paid close attention to the video. It was complicated stuff, and
she wanted to make sure she wasn't missing anything.

"*A series of tunnels are created below the body of ore,*" said the female narrator. "*V-shaped holes are blasted into the rock, creating funnels. Gravity then pulls the copper-laden rock down to the bottom of the funnels, where the weight of all that rock causes it to break up, crushing itself. Mounds of crushed rock are then scooped up from the bottom of each funnel, starting the process all over again. More ore falls into those funnels, and the cycle repeats.*"

When the lights came back on, the wire service reporter raised her hand. "Can block caving be done at any mine site?"

Leah sighed. The reporter hadn't done her homework. The block caving technique was the big new thing in the hard-rock mining industry.

Morgan looked pleased with the question and shook her head. "No, not at all. We lucked out. The rock conditions here were favorable for natural breakage. That doesn't happen at all sites. The company drilled more than a hundred test holes into the deposit to pull out core samples." Morgan, who sat perched on a stool, hopped up and said, "Which I'll show you now, if you'll follow me. But first, if any of you want coffee, please help yourself on the way out." A cheer went up as Morgan pointed to a small table set up as a coffee station.

Morgan disappeared out the door, and her heels could be heard clicking down a hall. Leah trotted after her, determined to find a moment alone with the woman.

"Hey, Morgan," Leah said, catching up to her.

"Oh, hey there," Morgan replied, as if surprised to see her. Morgan paused, looking past her. The others hadn't yet made it into the hall. She lowered her voice all the same. "I wanted to thank you. For what you did yesterday. That was nice of you, and that man."

Leah cleared her throat. "Of course. I heard you're taking the TV crew underground. I want to go too."

Morgan shook her head slowly but firmly. "I'm sorry. That just won't be possible. That was arranged by my predecessor and approved by corporate. I'm afraid I can't help you there." A moment later, she added, "As much as I'd like to."

Leah doubted it. The fewer reporters on the tour, the better for the company. It didn't take a genius to figure out why that news outlet had gotten the approval. It was a notorious climate change naysayer and a cheerleader for old-fashioned mining and manufacturing, no matter the cost to the environment. Leah's news organization was much more objective, though they were sometimes accused of being overly progressive.

Leah nodded at the cell phone clutched in Morgan's dainty hand. "You can call corporate. Explain the situation. I was specifically told there would be no underground tours, and now I'm finding out there is and that my organization is shut out. If you won't make the call, then give me the number of whoever we need to call at the company to get this cleared up, and I'll have my editor call."

Morgan peered nervously around her, and Leah glanced over her shoulder. The reporters had made it halfway up the long hall, talking amongst themselves, sipping coffee.

"Okay, I'll call," Morgan said. "But I'm not promising anything."

"Thank you. I'd hate to start off this story wondering if the company had something to hide."

Morgan gave her a long, stony stare, then ducked into an open room. Moments later, she returned, face tight. "We're a go." She turned on her heel and strode to the end of the hall, waving a hand over her head. "Okay, everyone. If you can just follow me to our next stop."

Leah was pleased but surprised it had been so easy. Her ex-husband often said people found her intimidating, but she'd always suspected the comment came loaded with subtext. She was sure he meant they found her *size* intimidating.

They passed through a door into a breezeway leading to another Quonset hut. Inside, it reminded Leah of a big-box store, or a Home Depot. They were surrounded by tall stacks of orange metal shelving holding long wooden crates.

Morgan stood next to one that was open and said, "As I mentioned, the company took more than a hundred core samples. This was nearly ten years ago, when the company was exploring how much copper was in the ore body. They determined there was more than enough copper to justify the massive investment required for block caving. And this is where all those core samples are cataloged and stored."

Leah began to fidget. So far, it was all *blah, blah, blah*. She could care less about core samples. The rest of the above-ground tour would be much of the same—mostly show, no tell. The heart of the operation was below ground, and she was anxious to get a firsthand look. But, like any tour guide, Morgan was going to stick to the script. Leah snapped a few photos of the vast room and the wooden crates with her phone.

The tour moved outside and dragged on for nearly an hour. Morgan proved herself adept at batting away the reporters' questions about safety.

"Mining is an inherently dangerous job," she said. "Which is why our safety protocols are the most rigorous in the industry."

Leah tried repeatedly to get Morgan on the record about the company's plan for dealing with the old tailings pond. Morgan sidestepped those.

"It's something we take very seriously. We've hired the best engineers, and they're developing a plan, which I can assure you will make the pond safe for the environment and for our local communities."

Leah cleared her throat. "That's what the company has been saying since the digging started six years ago, but it hasn't released any details. When, exactly, can we expect to see the final plan?"

Morgan didn't hesitate. "I don't have that information right now, but I'll get back to you by email." The young woman's face had taken on a mask-like quality.

It was obvious Leah's questions had annoyed Morgan—especially after she'd arranged for Leah to go down into the mine—but they each had their roles to play. It was just too bad Leah had to be the one to help her out of the Prestwich Squeeze. It must have been awkward—for the reporter who'd witnessed her panic attack to be taking her first big tour. Leah wondered how the hell Morgan was going to take them underground when she suffered so severely from claustrophobia.

Morgan ended the tour in the hoist control room. The group watched as an operator guided a cage, suspended from the big A-frame, deep into the earth. The cage was filled with miners starting their shift.

As word began to spread that some reporters were being allowed down into the mine, the ones who were left out protested. Leah leaned against a wall, waiting as an increasingly frazzled Morgan dealt with the turmoil. After ten minutes of wrangling and several calls to company headquarters, Morgan escorted everyone to a small wooden building, where she produced a stack of papers.

"These are waivers," she said. "Everyone needs to sign them before we go."

Leah read through hers quickly. It released the company from all liability in the event of accident or death, even if caused by any individual or the company. The waiver explained the risks in detail, including tripping and falling and damage to clothing and personal items. Death was mentioned in several places. The lawyer who'd written it had managed to clearly convey every dire possibility, while keeping it to one page.

"I can't sign this," one of the reporters said, glancing up with a look of alarm. It was the woman with the wire service.

Leah, standing closest to her, whispered, "It's pretty standard."

The woman pursed her lips and shook her head. "Our lawyers have told us never to sign anything while on a story." Straightening, she added, "Besides, I don't really need to go down there. The TV crew is shooting pool video."

Leah wanted to say, "Yes, you do," but it was none of her business.

In the end, the other reporters decided—for various reasons—not to sign the waiver and gave their contact information to the photographer. They left quickly after that, with some discussion of meeting for lunch in town. Morgan looked relieved.

Leah and the two-man news crew watched a short safety video, signed another form acknowledging they'd seen it, then went to a white-painted room, where they pulled on neon jackets and pants. They also donned boots, hardhats with headlamps, and safety harnesses.

Leah noted that Morgan didn't put on any of the gear, which made her wonder if the woman had arranged for someone else to take them underground. That would be unusual. PR types usually insisted on handling reporters themselves. They were halfway to the giant A-frame, boots grinding against gritty pavement, when Leah spotted a man walking toward them, suited up, hardhat in one hand. He waved at Morgan, who flicked her hair back at the sight of him.

The man was tall, well over six feet, with black curly hair. Even from that distance, Leah knew exactly who he was. She felt the frantic fluttering of a dozen butterflies in her stomach, and a jolt of adrenaline nearly made her dizzy.

It was Mig. Miguel Luna. The last she'd heard, he'd been working at a mine in Arizona, where he lived with his wife and two kids.

He stopped when he spotted her, smiling. "Leah."

Morgan rushed over to greet him, then spun around to face the small group, beaming. "This is Miguel Luna. He's our senior mining engineer, and he'll be taking over the next part of the tour."

Chapter 7

Leah held her breath when the blue sky faded from view and they plunged into darkness. The steel cage rattled as the group of four descended. She resisted the powerful urge to grab Mig's arm. They were standing close enough for her to get a whiff of the pine-scented soap he used. By some sort of unspoken understanding, after a slightly awkward embrace, they'd only had the briefest of polite exchanges.

"We went to high school together," Mig had told Morgan.

The moment Mig had appeared, Morgan's behavior had gone from all business to after-hours flirty. He'd always had that effect on women.

If it weren't for the experience of dropping a mile below the surface in a steel cage, Leah's knees would feel weak for other reasons.

Mig switched on his headlamp. Leah followed his example, as did the two men on the TV crew. The dancing light only added to the eeriness of the ride. Thank God she didn't suffer from claustrophobia, or she'd be in full-blown panic mode, and they hadn't even reached the bottom yet.

The reporter, Randall King, was talking into the camera, narrating his experience as the video rolled. Leah had to stand close to Mig to stay out of the shot. He winked and gave her arm a quick, reassuring pat. She stared down at his hand in surprise. It was large, thick, and brown. More importantly, it also lacked a wedding ring.

Not only had Miguel Luna returned to Tribulation Gulch, but he was also single.

So *that's* what her mother had been hinting at.

Then again, given the way she felt as her former high school boyfriend towered over her in the cage, her mother wasn't wrong. Leah hadn't seen Mig in more than two decades, and now, her hands itched with the desire to touch him. It was a good thing the descent was such a noisy, clanking ride, otherwise Mig might hear her heart slamming like a hammer against her chest.

She had to get a grip. They still had the rest of the tour to get through, and she needed to focus on the story and the mining operation, not Mig.

"How much longer?" Daniel, the photographer asked. His voice sounded strained.

Mig peered through the cage's steel mesh. "Another seven minutes or so. It takes fifteen minutes to get to the bottom, so we're halfway there."

"What were you looking at?" Leah asked.

"Markers on the wall," he said. "But I could just as easily have looked at my watch."

Unlike Morgan, Mig didn't keep up a running commentary. He couldn't, Leah concluded. At least, not without having to yell to be heard. Besides, Randall was talking into the camera again.

"I'd hate to know what my blood pressure is doing right now," he said at full volume. "And I can't imagine doing this journey twice a day, five days a week, to get to and from work.

It takes a different breed of man to work this far underground."

Mig leaned toward Leah. "You look great," he whispered, then winked again.

She suppressed a smile. Mig had always been bold. And taller. They'd burned brightly in high school and flamed out when they went their separate ways to college. No hard feelings, but some lingering regret on her part. The guys she'd met after Mig, including her ex-husband, lacked his humor and spark.

The air was getting warmer and more humid. A musty, damp smell became stronger the further they descended. When the cage finally lurched to a stop, Leah was gripped by a moment of dizziness and nausea. Mig held the steel door open, and they entered a low, covered walkway that was just tall enough for Mig to stand up straight. Leah heard a familiar sound ahead, like water dripping, but couldn't see it. Whatever was making the noise was around a corner.

Daniel, the photographer, exited first, walking backward while pointing the camera at Randall.

Mig's hand shot out, grabbing Daniel by the arm. "That not a safe thing to do down here," he said sternly. "You can film, but I need you to stand still while you do it."

Leah wriggled in her safety jacket, wishing she'd left her sweater behind. Despite the air blowing through vents on the wall, it was uncomfortably warm. Sweat trickled down her back.

Daniel followed Mig, camera perched on his shoulder. "Is that water?" he said loudly.

Mig stopped. "You might want to pull up your hoods until we reach our first stopping point." He pulled something from the pocket of his jacket and handed it to the photographer. It was a sheet of plastic. "And you'll want to cover your camera until we get through the next bit."

Leah was happy to take up the rear. It gave her a chance to study her gloomy surroundings. And Mig.

The humidity was stifling. They walked into a downpour—an underground downpour. It didn't make any sense. Warm water sprayed her face, and they sloshed through several inches of water on the floor. She hurried ahead to catch up with the others, who'd rounded a corner.

The group was bunched up in a dimly lit passageway. Mist rose into the air, fogging her safety glasses. Leah swiped them clear with a finger. Beyond Mig, bright lights marked where the passage widened. It was as hot and humid as a steam room, and she wondered why Mig had stopped in such an awkward spot.

"We're so far down that the rock in this area is warm from the earth's molten core," he said. "Miners call this hot spot 'The Devil's Hand,' and they usually scoot right past it, so that's what we should do too." He turned to Daniel and said, "I'm guessing you'll want to film that."

"We sure do," Randall said, stepping close to the rock wall. As soon as Daniel started shooting, Randall repeated what Mig had said. He did a few takes until he was satisfied.

Leah wiped her brow. Damp hair stuck to the sides of her neck, and she brushed it away. They left the narrow corridor.

"It's slippery around here, so watch your step," Mig cautioned over his shoulder.

Daniel was walking just ahead of her. He turned around and removed the earbud he used to monitor the camera's audio. "Did you say something?"

"No," she shouted, over the relentless whirring of the fans.

They walked beneath an arch made of steel beams into a passageway with a steel mesh ceiling. Eventually, the passageway opened into a wide tunnel. It was surprisingly roomy and lined with concrete. The air felt drier. A light coating of fine mud covered the floor, but it was better than all that standing water. Distant laughter came from farther down the tunnel, ricocheting off the walls—the sound of men going about their jobs, a mile underground. Leah wondered how they could stand it. Less than half an hour into the tour, she already yearned for blue sky.

Pipes bolted to the walls snaked along the tunnel. They stretched the length of the ceiling too, disappearing into the gloom. Skinny cables drooped in mysterious patterns along the walls. The whole place reminded Leah of the twisted corridors of a spaceship in an *Alien* movie.

Mig positioned himself next to a stack of white plastic bins with a handwritten sign that read: NON-POTABLE WATER. DO NOT DRINK! Leah thought the brownish color of the liquid inside served as warning enough. She couldn't imagine anyone wanting to drink that.

Mig rested an elbow atop one of the containers and waited until Daniel had adjusted his earbud and resumed filming. "You're probably wondering what was up with all the water back there. That's a little problem we discovered when we got down here. We had to fix it before we could continue. There's an aquifer above us that produces about six hundred gallons of water a minute, so we had to install two pumps and a bunch of pipe to carry the hot water back to the surface." He tipped his head back and pointed at the ceiling. "That's just some of the pipe."

Mig looked back down and caught Leah's eye. He licked his lips.

Leah rolled her eyes. *Grow up*, she mouthed.

"Why's it so noisy down here?" Randall asked.

"I hadn't noticed," Mig said, his expression serious. Then he grinned, teeth flashing white in his handsome face. "Just kidding. Those are fans. The normal temperature down here is one hundred and seventy degrees, so that's another thing we had to take care of. There are massive air conditioning units throughout the tunnels. Without them, we wouldn't be able to work down here."

Mig answered their questions easily enough but didn't elaborate. Leah suspected giving tours to reporters wasn't something he usually did. Randall seemed pleased enough with Mig's casual approach.

Daniel took the camera off his shoulder. His face looked pinched and drawn. He quickly glanced up, as if expecting something to drop from the ceiling onto his head.

The tour moved further down the tunnel, where Mig pointed to a conveyor belt leading to a hoisting shaft. He explained it was an example of the modern mechanization and automation that allowed the mine to run with a small crew. After a five-billion-dollar investment, it was important to keep operating costs low, and that meant operating with as few people as possible. But when asked about safety, Mig was no more forthcoming than Morgan had been.

"We're all about safety here," he said. "But if you want answers to any specific questions, I'm going to defer to Morgan to get you what you need."

Leah found that answer annoying but understandable. Mig was an engineer, not a press flack. If he said something conflicting with the company line, he'd have hell to pay.

They followed Mig further into the tunnel. Heavy equipment lined the walls. "As you know, operations don't start until tomorrow, and when they do, it'll be an entirely different scene down here…"

Leah's attention shifted to Daniel, who had his back turned, camera pointed at the wall. Randall was standing between his photographer and Mig. Neither man seemed to notice what Daniel was doing. Leah peered at the wall.

In dull, reddish paint, someone had written: I CURSE THIS PLACE.

The words took her breath away.

The same words The Copper Man had scrawled on the old trestle before he'd jumped into the tailings pond.

Those four words were no accident. Someone who worked for the new mining company had written them there, and recently enough that the message hadn't been painted over.

She couldn't imagine why anyone would write those words, unless someone knew about the media tour in advance and wanted to stir up trouble. Or maybe it was just a bit of weird miner humor, an old-timer trying to spook his co-workers. But that didn't make much sense either. The Copper Man killed himself thirty-five years ago. Most of the miners were probably too young to know much about the case.

A worker in a neon vest brushed past them. He had grizzled white eyebrows, a heavily lined face, and a strong smell of cigarettes.

"Those are popping up everywhere," he hissed at Leah. "You should look into it, and other stuff besides." He scurried past her, toward The Devil's Hand.

Leah slipped her phone out of her pocket and took some pictures.

When she'd finished, she noticed Daniel had squeezed his eyes shut and was shaking his head.

"You okay?" she asked.

Without responding, his eyes flew open, and he backed away quickly. She watched in alarm as he fled down the tunnel. Was he chasing after the miner for an interview? The young photographer hadn't gotten far, no more than a few yards, when he came to an abrupt stop, his free hand coming up to his ear.

The one with the earbud.

Leah wondered if it was acting up, sending feedback or static into his ear.

Daniel moved erratically, from one side of the tunnel to the other. Whatever was happening, it looked like more than a panic attack—a medical episode of some sort. The photographer ripped the hardhat from his head, eyes wild, mouth open and gasping for air.

Behind her, Mig's voice echoed down the corridor. "I need you to put that hardhat back on, Daniel. Immediately."

"What are you doing, Daniel?" Randall cried.

Leah stood between Daniel and the other two men. The hardhat slipped from his hand, his eyes glazed and unfocused. She was hurrying forward, when he lurched into motion, stumbling toward her, mouth opening wide, eyes round with panic. He careened past her, tripping. His arms windmilled as he fought to regain his balance. And then he was falling.

Daniel's head slammed into the corner of a long steel vat filled with murky water. He struck the edge with such force, his head seemed to bounce off it.

Leah heard herself scream.

"Jesus Christ," Mig cried, and then he was crouching next to Daniel.

Blood spurted from a wound gaping open from one side of Daniel's forehead to the other. Leah could see muscle and bone.

A miner came pounding from down the hall, took one look at Daniel, and said, "I'll call for help."

Shaking, Leah collapsed next to Mig, eyes trying to avoid the hideous injury. Daniel's chest wasn't moving.

Randall stood somewhere behind them, breathing raggedly. "What the hell just happened?"

Leah hardly heard him. A few minutes ago, Daniel had been alive and well. Now, he might be dead.

And by Mig's grim expression, that's what he thought too.

Debra Castaneda

Chapter 8

Daniel was dead. Leah had watched in stunned silence as the photographer's body was loaded into the cage.

After they'd given statements, a grim-faced safety supervisor escorted Leah and Randall out of the lobby, then turned on his heel and went back inside. Mig was holed up with Morgan in one of the Quonset huts.

Daniel's corpse would be taken to a hospital in Jackson, where the medical examiner would perform an autopsy. The small group of journalists clustered around Randall, who began to cry as he explained the accident to the satellite truck operator, a forty-something woman with short purple hair.

"I just can't believe it," she repeated. "Daniel was only twenty-seven. His birthday was just last week."

Randall's face had gone pasty white under his cap of caramel hair. He stood in front of the large vehicle, a hand pressed to his throat, and turned to Leah. "Do you want to sit down in the truck for a minute? To do social media, or whatever?"

She accepted, grateful to get out of the wind and into a quiet place to pull herself together. Her body felt alternately hot and cold, like a rock had settled in her belly. With heavy steps, she followed Randall into the satellite truck. It was cramped—barely room for two people. The walls were lined with screens. Lights flickered.

Randall gestured to a chair next to a shallow counter, then went outside to call his producer. She couldn't hear the exact words, but his anguished tone was clear enough.

Leah collapsed into the swivel chair and closed her eyes, trying to take deep calming breaths. She had work to do. Just because she'd witnessed a tragedy didn't mean she got a free pass.

The satellite truck operator climbed up the stairs. "You okay?"

Tears welled in Leah's eyes. "Not really."

The woman squeezed past her, crossed to the far end of the tiny control room, and opened a drawer. Leah watched as she pulled out a mug and a bottle of Glenlivet Scotch.

"My name is Crystal, and this is just for emergencies." She poured a generous amount of the pale golden liquid and set the mug in front of Leah.

Leah didn't hesitate. She drank it down, the silky vanilla sweetness sliding down her throat.

Crystal poured herself a shot and swallowed it. When Randall came in, eyes red, she gave him one too.

"They want me to send something in as soon as possible," he said to Crystal. "Can you shoot it?"

Leah's eyes widened. After the accident, she'd lost track of Daniel's camera. The last time she'd seen it, it was on the ground where he'd dropped it before he went sprawling to his death.

Randall retrieved a bag from outside the door. "Someone from the mine brought this out. He said it looks busted, but hopefully, the memory card is fine. I said I'd make a copy and give it to the safety guy."

"Maybe you should check with your producer first," Leah said. "They might want to talk to a lawyer about that."

Randall rubbed a hand over his face. "Thanks. You're right. I'm still not thinking straight."

Crystal pulled a camera from a metal bin, and they disappeared outside, the door slamming behind them. The Scotch was doing its job—Leah was over the worst of the shakiness. She grabbed her phone.

Her first text was to Sue, her editor, telling her about the accident, followed by brief posts to social media. When she was done, she typed a short news story on her phone, proofed it, and when she was satisfied, emailed it to Sue, who'd post it on the company accounts. The story contained just the facts. No speculation. She made no mention of Daniel's odd behavior in the tunnel, or the bizarre way he'd fallen.

As if he had been pushed, except there was no one standing near him.

Leah also left out the message scrawled on the walls of the mine: I CURSE THIS PLACE.

She'd decide how to handle all that later, when she had more time to think and her head didn't feel like it was stuffed with cotton. While she still had WiFi, Leah emailed the photos she'd taken of the mine tour to the producer at the cable news show to use during her afternoon guest slot.

When she was done, she thanked Randall and Crystal, who said they were staying at a hotel in Tribulation Gulch. They exchanged phone numbers and said goodbye.

Leah spent the next hour staking out the lower dirt lot where the mine workers parked. The morning shift had just ended, and men were trickling out. She attempted to talk to a few of them, but those who paused long enough to listen just shook their heads and hurried to their cars. A few men strode past her, eyes firmly on the ground, pretending they didn't see her.

A cold wind had kicked up, blowing over the Dinky Minors. She wondered when northwest Wyoming would get the message summer was around the corner. Leah grabbed a down jacket from the back of the Blazer, put it on, and waited. It was almost one thirty. Past her usual lunch time, but she wasn't hungry—not after seeing that horrendous wound on Daniel's head and all that blood.

She couldn't hang out much longer. Leah needed to get home in time for her TV appearance. She'd already done a test call to make sure her mother's internet was fast enough. TV people could obsess about video quality.

Leah leaned against the Blazer, trying unsuccessfully to get someone on the mine crew to talk to her and starting to wonder if she was wasting her time.

She was reaching into her pocket for her car keys when two men appeared. They stopped when they spotted her, and she waved.

Both were pushing sixty, with the tight builds of men who spent their days doing manual labor. One had a faded yellow beard and mustache. The other had a grizzled ring of hair on top of his head. Instead of strolling past, they exchanged nervous looks and slowly approached her.

"Are you here about the accident?" the bearded man asked.

"Yes and no," Leah said. "I was down in the mine when it happened. In fact, I saw it."

The man with the hair donut brightened. "Were you with those TV people? I watch that network all the time."

She shook her head. "I'm a reporter, but I don't work with them. Would you mind if I asked you a few questions?"

The bearded man frowned. "You said you saw the accident. We weren't even there. I don't know how we could help you."

Leah stepped a little closer, zipping up her jacket. The wind was blowing her hair around, and she pushed it from her face. "While I was in the tunnel, I saw something I'd like to ask you about."

The grizzled man began shaking his head. "Oh, here we go. If it's about all that graffiti nonsense, I don't want to get involved."

Leah's heart beat a little faster. So, the miner who'd approached her underground was telling the truth.

"You don't need to give me your names. I'm just looking for a little background information. It's not something the company wants to talk about." She gave them a pleading look. Leah watched as the two men exchanged uneasy glances. "Please," she added, shoving her phone into a pocket. "No names. No notes. Just you and me having a little chat."

"I guess we can do that," the bearded man said grudgingly. "My name is Joe. Just don't use it, like you said."

"I won't," she promised with a reassuring smile.

The other man gave a defeated sigh. "I'm Ron."

Leah glanced around. A small group of men had entered the lot and were now staring at them. She had to hurry before someone called security.

"What can you tell me about this graffiti?"

With discomfort, Ron looked down at his feet for a few moments before answering. "Well, it's the same thing over and over again."

"'I curse this place,' is what it says," Joe cut in. "You probably have no idea what it means. You're too young for that, so I'll tell you. We had some murders around here a long time ago. Kids, each and every one of them. And the guy who did it worked here." Fingernails black with dirt, he pointed in the direction of the old trestle. "But he killed himself before they caught him, is what happened, and he wrote 'I curse this place' on that bridge, where he jumped into the tailings pond."

Ron nodded. "That's right. So, then those tunnels get dug, and guys start going down there, and it ain't long before they start getting spooked. And it's not just that graffiti. Now, guys are coming out saying they've seen shadows and heard stuff, usually when they're all alone." He paused, mouth pursed. "Some people can't take being underground like that."

Joe rubbed the back of his neck as if it ached. "That's when the accidents started happening. Nothing too serious, mind you. Just the sort of stuff that tends to happen when people aren't paying attention. Heavy machinery mistakes, slips and falls, things like that. Some fellow broke his back, but he was a contractor, and he wasn't wearing a harness like he was supposed to."

"Do you have any idea who might be responsible for the graffiti?" Leah asked. "Or why they're doing it?"

Joe gave his beard a thoughtful tug. "You got me. But once those guys have had a few whiskeys, they'll tell you, no problem. They think it's the ghost of The Copper Man come back to haunt the place."

Leah's eyes snapped open. "You're kidding?"

Ron grinned, teeth stained dark by nicotine. "He ain't kidding. Come on, now. Wyoming is famous for ghost towns. My wife bought this book about haunted places. I haven't read it myself, but she says it's real good, and it's all about ghosts in Wyoming. There was nothing in it about The Copper Man, though." He gave a disappointed shrug.

Joe jabbed Ron in the side, then jerked his head in the direction of the men at the other end of the parking lot, watching.

"We ought to get going," Joe said.

Ron nodded. "Yeah, we ought."

Leah watched them walk to their trucks, shoulders hunched against the wind. She got in the Blazer and headed home, mulling over their strange story.

Debra Castaneda

Chapter 9

A plumber's van was parked in front of the house. When Leah walked into the kitchen, her mother and Harper were sitting at the table, making tiny trees out of sticks and cotton. There was fluffy green stuff everywhere, and her daughter had brown paint on her cheeks.

"Look, Mom!" Harper said, holding up a tree.

Leah forced herself to give it her full attention. Ever since she'd gone back to work full-time two years ago—after her divorce—her daughter had become especially sensitive to any signs her mother was distracted.

"It's perfect." She kissed the top of Harper's head.

"They better be," her mother said. "We've made enough of them for a whole forest."

The door to the basement opened, and a man appeared, breathing heavily. He had ruddy cheeks and an enormous double chin. "All right, Mrs. Shaw, I've got some good news and some bad news. Which do you want first?"

Patricia stared at him over the top of her tortoiseshell reading glasses. "Just give it to me straight, Don."

Don took another step into the kitchen, holding a wrench in one hand and a limp rag in the other. "Well, I can't find anything wrong. Not a thing. And after running a bunch of water, I'm not seeing the funny color you saw. The toilet tanks look fine. I checked the exposed pipe in the basement, and that looks fine too. But those iron pipes are old and need to be replaced. That's what I'm recommending. I'll come up with an estimate and drop it by when it's ready."

Leah's mother groaned. "That's going to cost a fortune. Isn't there anything you can do?"

Don shook his head, double chin wagging with a life of its own. "It's the cost of owning these beauties," he said, patting the wall. "Now look, if that funny color comes back, try and capture it in the tub or the sink so I can take a look for myself."

Once the plumber had gone, Patricia said, "I don't know if I trust that man."

Leah grabbed a bottle of water from the fridge and drank it down in long gulps. "That's what you always say, but you never hire anyone else."

"Don's the only plumber in Tribulation Gulch. The other guy moved to Jackson Hole."

Leah glanced at the clock. Forty-five minutes until her TV appearance. Just time enough to eat a little something and put on some makeup while she drank a cup of hot tea. But first, she needed to have a quiet word with her mother. "Can I borrow Gimme for a few minutes?" she said to Harper.

Harper looked up, frowning. "Okay. But don't take forever because we need to put the trees in, and I'm going to Shelley's tonight."

Leah planned to cover the community meeting at the high school, and she'd forgotten her mother had decided to come also. The meeting was about the mine, so Patricia wanted to attend "as a stakeholder." She'd arranged to have her granddaughter spend the evening with Shelley Palmer, who lived around the block and was thrilled to have Harper over. Shelley was Patricia's oldest friend. They'd known each other since they both lived in Utah, where their husbands had worked for the Kennecott copper mine.

In the living room, Leah stumbled through the story of what happened to the photographer in the mine.

"But why did he take off his hardhat?" Patricia cried.

"I don't know, Mom. He just…did."

"Was he goofing around, or on drugs?" her mother pressed. "You know young people these days."

"Mom, he wasn't a kid. He was a professional." She hesitated, running a hand through her hair. It was a tangled mess from the wind. "I don't know. Maybe he wasn't feeling well or something. Maybe if something was wrong, it'll come out in the autopsy."

Her mother stared down at Harper's fairy world. It had expanded beyond the coffee table and was taking over an end table. When Leah and Liam were little, they weren't allowed to play in the living room. Or leave their toys anywhere downstairs, for that matter.

"Do they still plan to open tomorrow?" Patricia asked.

"I think so. I asked the safety engineer. He said since it appeared that it was an accidental fall, it was pretty straightforward, and they'd be cleared to open. Maybe that's something we'll find out tonight."

Leah was exhausted just thinking about the meeting. The mine was a contentious local issue, with feelings running high. The meeting was sure to drag on, but it was something she couldn't afford to miss. All she wanted to do was have a nice dinner, drink a bunch of wine, and crawl into bed. Maybe even bribe Harper into snuggling under the covers and watching a Disney movie.

She went upstairs, washed her face, and put on her makeup, going heavy on the eyeliner and mascara and brushing brown gel on her eyebrows. For the finishing touch, she added a swipe of Nearly Nude across her lips, then surveyed the results, pleased. Professional. Serious. Not exactly glamorous, but attractive enough.

Her hair was still a mess. She spritzed it with curl enhancing spray, combed her fingers through it, and scrunched. Her hair cooperated by falling into loose waves around her face.

Before she went live, she had a brief conversation with the producer and made it clear she couldn't elaborate on the details of the accident. When the interview got underway, she gave an involuntary shudder, recounting the descent in the cage, and shivered when she explained what it was like so far under the earth. The segment went smoothly, but she was glad when it was over. She always found being on the air draining, but it was worth the stress. The appearance fees made a big difference in the quality of her life, and Harper's.

The network had approached her about a permanent reporting job recently. It paid more, nearly double what she was making, but she was still undecided. They wanted her to be on camera every day, which meant showing more than just her shoulders and face. Her body didn't fit conventional standards. And while she was able to handle any "big and tall" comments that came her way, she wasn't sure she was ready for a career in front of the camera and the inevitable ugly comments on social media.

After a quick dinner of turkey burgers and the ever-present salad, Leah made a pot of coffee and poured it into two thermoses: one for herself, one for her mother.

Shelley lived around the block, in a brick cottage painted white. Lights blazed from behind frilly curtains. The cottage had an exaggerated peaked roof and a robin's-egg-blue door. The inside was as adorable as the outside, with built-in bookcases, a wood beam ceiling, and Dutch doors throughout. It was like a storybook house come to life. Harper came to an abrupt stop just inside the doorway, eyes wide, entranced. She didn't seem to notice the two other children seated cross-legged in front of the fireplace, playing with a pile of Legos, or the tall man standing in a corner.

It was Mig. And presumably, those were his kids, both about Harper's age.

The little boy gave a tentative wave.

Shelley rushed toward Leah. She looked every bit the librarian she was, with silver hair cut in a pixie and black-framed glasses.

"Leah!" she cried. "How wonderful to see you, and you *look* wonderful!" Her eyes traveled to Harper, who was scowling at the children. "And Harper! I made Rice Krispy Treats, and we're going to have hot chocolate too. I'm so happy you'll be keeping me company while your mom and grandma go to that boring meeting."

"Her name is Gimme," Harper said sternly.

Behind her, Leah's mother said, "Harper! You mind your tone, young lady." Patricia sounded more amused than annoyed.

Leah's heart sank. It wasn't a promising start to the night. If she had known about the other kids, she would have warned Harper, given her a chance to adjust to the idea.

Shelley glanced at Leah and shot her a reassuring smile that said *no big deal.*

Harper pointed at the children, so close in age they had to be twins. "Why are *they* here?"

Leah could feel Mig staring at her. She mouthed, *Sorry.* He grinned in return.

Shelley clapped her hands once. "I'm a terrible hostess because I should have introduced everyone already. Harper, there was a little change of plans. It was just going to be the two of us, but my neighbor had to go to that same meeting as your mom and your Gimme, and he asked me if I could look after Sofia and Mason. So now, you'll have company!"

Patricia tapped Harper on the shoulder. "Harper, what do you say to your new friends?"

"They're not my friends," Harper protested. "I don't even know them!"

Before Leah could respond, Mig detached himself from the corner and strode across the room. He knelt in front of Harper.

"Hi, Harper. My name is Miguel Luna, and I'm their dad. You're not going to believe this, but I'm also an old friend of your mom's. We went to school together, and we used to have lots of fun." He looked up at Leah and winked. "Didn't we, Leah?"

Leah felt her mother jab her in the ribs. She managed a stiff nod.

Mig continued. "So, since we got along, that means you kids will too. Right?" Both children had their father's dark curly hair.

Leah held her breath as Harper studied him, mouth puckered. It was an odd bit of logic that Mig had just presented, and Harper wasn't easily persuaded.

74

"Okay," Harper finally said, then went to join Sofia and Mason in front of the fire.

Leah's insides melted with relief. She watched Harper set Chicken aside and begin inspecting the buildings the children had made.

"Do you want to make the outhouse?" Mason asked.

"What's that?" Harper said.

As Sofia explained, a smile came to Harper's face. Leah relaxed even more.

Her mother whispered, "Let's go while the going is good."

Shelley flapped her hands at them. "Shoo, shoo, we'll be fine."

Leah had no doubt of that. Shelley seemed to be a highly capable woman. At the door, Leah said goodbye to her daughter, who gave a quick wave before accepting a pile of Legos from Mason.

In the cool evening air, they walked to her mother's white Suburban, Miguel beside them.

"Your kids seem so sweet," Leah said.

"Mostly," Miguel replied, sounding pleased. "They're twins, and sometimes, they can be in their own little world. I was in a bit of a panic about tonight, but I ran into Shelley, and she offered to watch them." He paused. "I hope that's okay."

Leah looked at him in surprise. "Of course. Why wouldn't it be?"

She heard the car door slam. Her mother had climbed into the SUV and started the engine.

Mig shrugged. "I don't know. It's just…you know…kinda weird. After all this time."

"It's not weird unless we make it weird."

Mig grinned. "Then we should definitely go out." His shoulders sagged. "But first, I've got to survive this meeting. I've gone to one before but just as an observer. This time, I'll be the official representative since Morgan…" His words drifted off, and he grimaced.

"Did they fire her?" Leah guessed.

"If I tell you, you can't write about it."

"Off the record. I promise."

"They fired her, all right. As soon as they found out she wasn't there when the accident happened. I was part of the group that interviewed Morgan during the hiring process, and she didn't say anything about having claustrophobia. Obviously, leading tours underground is a big part of the job, but apparently, that's not something she'd done in her previous jobs. I think she was expecting nothing but desk work. She told me she'd explained the situation to her boss, and he said it was okay for me to take the media folks underground. But she lied. Corporate knew nothing about it."

"Oh my God. That's terrible."

Mig sighed. "Yeah. I hardly know her, but I have to say, I'm a little worried. After they gave her the axe, she freaked out and couldn't stop crying, and then she had a panic attack or something, and someone had to drive her home."

Leah remembered the young woman's meltdown in the Prestwich Squeeze. Getting fired from a brand-new job certainly qualified as a traumatic experience. It also had to be humiliating. Morgan might be too embarrassed to call friends or family for support. She was all alone in a strange new town.

"Do you have her number?" Leah asked. "Can you call her?"

"I've tried, but she's not picking up. She said she found a place in town, but I don't know where."

The Suburban's horn blared, making them both jump. Through the windshield, Patricia scowled at Leah.

"I'll see you at the meeting," Mig said, then hurried toward his truck.

Chapter 10

On their way into the school auditorium, Leah pulled Mig aside. "I'm here to cover this story, and I might need to ask you an uncomfortable question or two. But just to be clear, it's not personal."

Mig's eyebrows shot up. "I think I'm actually disappointed. I'd prefer something personal." He disappeared inside, leaving her to stare after him, warmth flushing through her body despite the chilly mountain air.

About fifty people were clustered in several groups, talking. Leah needn't have bothered to bring coffee. There was plenty of it on a table at the back of the room, and homemade desserts too. She was reaching for a slice of pound cake when Patricia sidled up.

"Mary Guise makes those," her mother said. "With all the butter she uses, those have to be a thousand calories a slice."

Leah shot her mother a dark look, but her mother was looking at Mig a few yards away.

"He's in good shape, isn't he?"

Sneaking a glance in his direction, Leah had to agree. He'd put on weight since high school, but who hadn't? It suited him, and with his broad shoulders and tight waist, it was obvious he worked out.

"I guess," Leah said, snatching her hand back from the cake. She wandered off to the back row, dragged a folding chair to the wall, and sat. From that angle, she'd have a good view of the meeting and all its attendees. There was already some chatter about the fatal accident at the mine, but when people heard it involved a visitor, not a mineworker, and it was simply a fall, they soon moved on to other topics.

The room had split into two camps: the pro-mine people on the right, the anti-mine contingent on the left. Leah wondered if that had been intentional and smiled at the thought.

Most of the attendees were dressed in jeans and fleece pullovers. Except, of course, for her mother, who wore black pants, a white shirt with pearls, and a gray wool jacket. She sat front and center, surrounded by her pro-mine cronies from the business district.

At seven o'clock, the owner of Hook 'Em took the podium. Colt had to speak loudly because the microphone wasn't working. He wore a down vest over a checked shirt and a baseball cap with the fishing shop's logo. If the meeting didn't go his way, at least he'd get some free advertising out of it, Leah thought.

Mig sat in the second row. He turned, eyes scanning the room until he spotted her, then smiled and winked.

Leah tried not to stare at the back of Mig's curly head, or the occasional profile when he turned to speak to the man next to him.

Colt motioned for the first speaker to join him at the podium, introducing him as Gabriel Russo, rattled off his pedigree, which included engineering and environmental planning degrees, then thanked him for traveling from Berkeley, where he taught in the engineering department at the University of California.

The mention of the college elicited hisses and boos from the right side of the room.

Russo gave a good-natured smile and said, "I'm very glad to be here. Thank you for having me."

Like Colt, Russo was bald—or "bulbed," as Harper called it. Whether it was by nature or razor, it was impossible to tell these days. Either way, it suited him. Instead of a full beard like Colt, Russo sported a goatee.

For nearly twenty minutes, Russo explained the risks of hard-rock mining and the block caving method, and when someone shouted, "We've heard all this before, professor," Russo switched on a slide show.

After the lights had dimmed, Russo ran through the slides—mostly photos of mining disasters from around the world. Each one was accompanied by a brief description. The collapse of tailings dams, rivers tainted by toxic runoff, and lots and lots of dead fish.

A hush came over the audience. Leah suspected Russo knew exactly what he was doing when he'd chosen which disasters to highlight. If there was one thing that united the locals, it was their love for and reliance on Tribulation River.

The series of horrific photos came from all over the world: Spain, China, the Philippines, South Africa, and Italy. Leah scanned the room and saw heads shaking on both sides of the aisle.

"Those weren't all copper mines," Patricia said. "So, I'm not sure how all of that is applicable here." Cheers went up from the right side of the auditorium.

"Fair enough," Russo said mildly. "But that tailings dam you've got up at your mine can breach just as easily as any of those I've shown you, and if it does, it's going to send a whole lot of toxic sludge into the creek just beyond it, killing everything downstream. And just remember, seismic activity is common in these parts. You can have twenty to thirty earthquakes a month in Wyoming. Most are too small to feel, but you've got a significant fault running through the Absaroka Range. If I were you, I'd be worried about that." He paused. "Very worried."

And with that, Russo thanked the group for listening and sat down.

Colt got to his feet, introducing Miguel Luna as the spokesperson for the New Prestwich Mining Company. Mig got up and gripped the sides of the podium, cleared his throat, then launched into a brief explanation of that day's fatal accident involving a visiting member of the broadcast media. To Leah's surprise, not even the anti-mine group had any questions. But she did.

"Miguel," she called from the back of the room.

His eyes snapped open. "Yes?"

She stood and pushed her shoulders back. "I'm Leah Shaw, with *America Today News*. I understand there have been other accidents at the mine since the project started. Can you tell us where they've occurred? Above ground? Below ground?"

People turned in their chairs and stared. She lifted her chin and ignored them.

Mig coughed and took a sip of water. "Unfortunately, accidents at mining sites aren't unusual. They happen. Both above and below ground. I can't give you a breakdown, but I can tell you that each accident was immediately reported to the Mine Safety and Health Administration. A few have been injuries causing lost workdays. Those usually involved operator error and heavy equipment. We've had more minor injuries without workdays lost. All of those are included in quarterly reports that you can view online. We haven't had any fatalities." His mouth twitched. "Until today. Fatal accidents are included in fatality reports. The MSHA investigates each incident, as it will with this one."

She knew all that already but needed him on the record for her story. "Thank you," she said, then took her seat.

Colt, standing with arms crossed in front of his chest, addressed the room. "We have several items on our agenda we'd like to have Miguel address. So, let's start off with the issue that concerns us most, and that's the tailings dam and how the company plans to make it safe."

Mig repeated the same thing Morgan told reporters earlier that day. The company was working on it, and as soon as the plan was ready, they would present it to the community.

Leah got to her feet again. "The company bought the property more than ten years ago. If it can dig tunnels a mile deep in that time frame, certainly it could formulate a plan to deal with the tailings pond."

Mig's eyebrows shot up. He stared at her for a long moment before answering. "Tailings are complicated. The plan involves serious engineering, and this is something we don't want to rush. We've got to get it right."

"What about Professor Russo's concerns about seismic activity?" she pressed. "What if there's an earthquake between now and whenever the company produces a plan, plus however long it takes to fix the problem? The dam could fail." Leah sat, never taking her eyes off Mig.

His face had taken on a mask-like quality.

"Then we're all fucked," Colt said loudly.

"Language!" Patricia admonished from the second row.

Mig rubbed his temple. "I can assure you that we are working on it, as fast as we can. In the meantime, we're shoring it up until a more permanent solution is found."

Russo waved his hand above his head. "Shoring it up with more tailings and waste materials!"

Mig hesitated, jaw tightening. "Those are the materials we have available, so yes. But as I said, it's temporary."

Russo stood and faced the room. "It's just more of the same toxic stuff. The only thing that's going to work, to prevent a disaster, is reinforced concrete."

"As I said, we're using available materials as the most expedient and temporary solution until a safe, permanent solution is found," Mig said stiffly.

Leah thought he was doing well as fill-in flack, considering. Mig was an engineer, not a public relations official trained to handle tough questions.

The meeting lasted another hour. Mig took questions about the promised widening of the Prestwich Tunnel and surprised everyone by saying the construction plan would be ready to present the following month. Mig had one last surprise announcement—the mining company had purchased several apartment complexes on the edge of town and planned to convert them into affordable housing for their workers.

Leah's hand shot up. "And when will those be ready?"

"Three months," Miguel said, smiling. "Tops."

Soon after that, the meeting ended. Mig was waiting for her just outside the door, hands shoved into his jacket pockets.

"That was beginning to feel personal," he said.

Under the outdoor lights, he looked tired and older. She wondered who took care of his kids while he was at work, but now was not the time to get into all that. The parking lot was empty. Most people had already left. A few, including her mother, remained inside after cornering the professor from Berkeley.

Leah shrugged. "Sorry, not sorry."

Mig tapped her on the shoulder. "You don't scare me."

"Maybe you should be a little scared," she said. That came out flirtier than she intended.

Mig flashed a roguish smile. "We should have dinner sometime. You know, catch up."

"With the kids?"

Mig grimaced. "Hell no. Mine are terrible at restaurants. I'll ask Shelley if she can babysit."

For once, Leah didn't have a snappy comeback. She hadn't expected to see Mig, of all people, in Tribulation Gulch. She also hadn't expected to experience even the faintest flicker of desire ever again, not after the series of dating disasters following her divorce from the man who left her for a younger woman. In fact, she'd vowed to take a break from men.

When she didn't answer, he tapped her shoulder again. "It's the least you can do, after cutting my balls off in there."

"Okay," she said.

Her face held a frown, but butterflies danced in her stomach.

Chapter 11

For once, Harper didn't resist going to bed. Playing with Sofia and Mason had tired her out. Harper thawed quickly, Shelley had said, and after they'd finished building the Lego fort, they ran around playing hide and seek, then finished off the plate of Rice Krispy Treats.

Leah could hardly believe it. Harper didn't make new friends easily. It was a process that usually took a full school year, with a lot of encouragement and play dates.

After helping a sleepy Harper brush her teeth, Leah tucked her into bed. "Do you want me to read you a story?"

Harper rolled over, yawning. "Not tonight, Mom. Night, night."

"No wandering around if you wake up, okay?"

Harper didn't respond. By her steady breathing, Leah could tell she'd already fallen asleep. The second miracle of the night.

Downstairs, it was her mother's turn to astound her. Patricia had opened a bottle of red wine. Two glasses, with generous pours, sat on a side table not yet commandeered by Harper's fairy world.

"What brought this on?" Leah asked, collapsing onto the sofa.

Her mother picked up a glass and handed it to her. "It sounds like you had a heck of a day. First, that terrible accident in the mine. And I just can't get over seeing you on TV. You were so good. Where in the world did you learn to do that?"

To Leah's surprise, her mother sounded impressed.

"Thank you." She took a sip. It was nice and smooth and probably cost a lot more than twelve dollars, her usual limit. "It just kind of happened. The show needed an environmental reporter to give some background on a breaking story, so I gave them an interview. And then they kept asking."

Patricia wrinkled her nose, glass in mid-air. "I don't like that network, though. Nothing but hand-wringing, bleeding-heart liberals. They're too extreme for me. Why don't you get on that other show? The one I watch?"

Leah nearly choked on her wine. "I don't think they'd have me."

"You don't know if you don't ask." Her mother gave her a sly look, one that helped Leah guess what was coming. "How is it seeing Miguel after all these years?" Her mother still pronounced it "M*ee*-gell."

"Weird. I know he's divorced, but I don't know much else. Do you know why the kids aren't with his ex?"

"Well, as I understand it, the kids were supposed to be with her, but she had to go back to Mexico when her mother went into hospice. So, Miguel has the children. Which isn't great timing, with the mine just starting up and all the hours they're putting in over there."

"Who's taking care of the kids?"

"Shelley helped him find someone. A friend of hers runs a daycare out of her home. If he needs to work late, Shelley helps out. She says they're such sweet kids and that Miguel is a very attentive father." Her mother finished the last of her wine and set the glass aside. "And by the way, it was so hectic when you got home, I forgot to mention it. I had the locksmith come out to fix Liam's door. Harper won't be getting in there anymore. I put the key under the runner on the hall table in case you need it."

Leah nodded. It's where the key had always been, but she didn't feel like talking about Liam's room. Not now—exhausted and pleasantly woozy from the wine. She washed the glasses while her mother checked the doors, then they went upstairs.

Before climbing into bed, Leah decided another shower was in order. Her neck and shoulders ached, and her skin was tacky after sweating it out in the mine. She let the water run to make sure it was clear before stepping under the nozzle, then let the hot spray hit her back.

As she padded to her bedroom, dressed in her robe, her hand slipped into the pocket, feeling around for the copper nugget that had appeared out of nowhere that morning. Until now, she'd forgotten all about it.

It wasn't there.

She checked the other pocket. Still nothing.

That morning, before she'd dressed and left for the mine tour, she'd hung the robe on a hook on the back of the door as usual. The nugget couldn't have fallen out on its own. Someone had to have taken it. Possibly, her mother. Maybe it upset her so much she'd thrown it out.

Leah went downstairs and knocked on her mother's door. Patricia had already changed into her pajamas. She was the only woman Leah knew who still wore matching tops and bottoms. Tonight's were cream satin with black piping. Her mother was sitting on the edge of the bed, rubbing lotion onto her hands. The room smelled of vanilla.

"Did you take the copper nugget we found today?" Leah asked.

Patricia shook her head. "No," she said slowly. "Why?"

"It's gone."

"But you put it in your pocket. I saw you. It's not there?"

Leah sighed. "Maybe Harper took it."

"Maybe," Patricia said with a little shrug. "She may have wanted it for her fairy world. Ask her in the morning."

Leah nodded and closed the door behind her. Her mother was probably right. The copper nugget hadn't sprouted wings and flown out of her pocket. But still, it nagged at her. If Harper had taken it, it had to be somewhere in her room.

Leah tiptoed inside, wincing every time the floorboards creaked beneath her feet. With the hall light on, the room wasn't completely dark. She could see Harper's huddled form on the bed. Gently running her hands over the top of the dresser, the nightstand, and the upholstered chair, Leah found no copper nuggets, just a few of Harper's hair ties and the books she'd brought from Denver.

Harper's head rested on the mattress, so she slid her hand under the pillow. Sometimes, Harper liked to keep "treasures" there, but there was nothing.

She was halfway to the door when Harper said, "Mom?" so loudly Leah's heart nearly exploded in her chest.

"I thought you were asleep!" she gasped.

Harper sniffed, clutching Chicken. Her legs dangled off the side of the bed. "You woke me up."

Leah sighed. For once, Harper had gone straight to sleep, and instead of relishing every peaceful moment, she woke her daughter up.

"I'm sorry, sweetie," she said, hurriedly tucking her back into bed. "I was just looking for something is all, and I thought you might have it."

Harper blinked at her in the dim light. "What?"

"That thing we found today. The copper nugget. You didn't see it, did you?"

"Uh uh," Harper said with an enormous yawn. "Can you go now, Mom?"

"Of course, sweetie. I'm sorry for waking you up."

Leah padded back to her room, mystified. The damn thing had to be *somewhere*. Maybe it had fallen out of her robe after all. She crawled on the floor, checking under the bed, the dresser, the end tables, and the low chair in the corner of the room. Unlike her own place, she didn't encounter a single dust bunny. She wondered how her mother kept up with such a big house.

Leah got to her feet with a groan. She was tired. Finding the copper nugget wasn't urgent, but she knew she wouldn't be able to sleep until she found it.

She bit her lip, thinking. *It's here. Somewhere.*

Liam's room. She knew it was there, felt the certainty of it in her bones. The thought made her dizzy. There was a faint buzzing in her ears.

With trembling fingers, she fumbled under the table runner and snatched up the key. She unlocked Liam's door, flicked on the lights, and stepped inside. Her heart was pounding so hard she could hear it in her ears. Her eyes swept the room and landed on Liam's toy chest.

The lid was open.

She didn't move for several moments, listening. The house was quiet. No footsteps in the hall. She crept forward, the hair on the back of her neck rising.

Holding her breath, she peered inside.

The copper nugget was there, sitting on top of the cowboy hat Liam wore on his last Halloween.

Chapter 12

When Leah woke, the copper nugget was sitting on the nightstand next to her bed, exactly where she left it. The mystery of how it ended up in Liam's toy chest had tormented her through the night. As she'd lain in bed, listening to the sounds of the old house creaking and groaning, her mind had swung in the wildest directions.

A ghost haunted the house.

Or was it poltergeists that liked to move things around?

Her thoughts kept returning to her brother. Maybe his spirit had returned, lured by the presence of another child.

But with the bright light of day streaming through the windows, the sound of her mother and daughter laughing in the kitchen, the smell of bacon drifting up the stairs, all of that seemed ridiculous. She'd imagined a worst-case scenario, and a supernatural one at that.

It didn't take a genius to figure out what was going on. She'd witnessed a horrible accident and had a surprise encounter with her high school boyfriend, which elicited all kinds of feelings. Leah had read an article once about catastrophic thinking. That's exactly what had happened— she'd fallen victim to completely irrational thoughts.

As she dressed, she concluded that Harper had done it. Harper connected the copper nugget with her deceased uncle and had wanted to return it to his room. So, before the locksmith arrived to fix the lock, Harper had found the copper nugget in the pocket of her mother's robe, slipped into Liam's room, and placed it in the toy chest, then forgotten to close the lid.

Leah had no intention of spoiling the morning by interrogating Harper or bothering her mother with it. It wasn't a big deal, and she didn't need to make it one.

Her phone chimed. A message had arrived from Rhonda Jones, her producer at the cable network. She wanted to know if Leah would file a story using the pool video from the underground mine tour. Leah's hands went clammy at the thought. She'd never done a TV story before, but more importantly, she didn't have a photographer or the pool video.

That wasn't the only message. Another had come in while she'd been in the bathroom. It was from Crystal, the purple-haired satellite truck operator. Crystal had emailed her a link to a site where she could download the video.

Leah fired up her laptop and confirmed it was in her inbox.

With a sigh, Leah called Rhonda. It would be much easier to discuss it over the phone.

"I'd love to help you out," Leah said, "but I just don't know how I can—"

"I've got it all figured out," said Rhonda. "You met Crystal, right? Well, she's a freelancer who works for us too. She's available to shoot and edit the piece, and she'll coach you through being on camera. Crystal's done some field producing for us, so it's perfect. And come on. How many times have I said you need to quit your other lame job and join us full time?"

"Only about a hundred times."

Leah realized she needed to get over herself. TV reporting wasn't rocket science. She could do it if she tried. And the money was better than what she was making now. A *lot* better.

"Okay," Leah said. "What do you want me to do?"

"First of all, put on your TV makeup…and take your makeup kit with you in case Crystal thinks you need more. I've just emailed you a few sample scripts. Look at those and copy the format. Do you think you can write something now and send it back to me as soon as possible? Once it's approved, you can either print out your script and take it with you, or you can do what a lot of reporters do and have it on your phone."

Leah swallowed. The average TV story, the kind Rhonda was talking about, was around two minutes. Her pieces for her online publication were much longer.

You can handle two minutes, she told herself.

"This is great, Leah!" Rhonda gushed. "You're going to do great! I want you to watch that pool video, take notes on what you want to use, and then when you write, be sure your narration explains what people are seeing. It's called 'writing to video.'" Rhonda paused, laughing. "Oh my god, we're trying to cram a whole semester of broadcast writing into a phone conversation."

Rhonda spent another fifteen minutes explaining what she needed in more detail.

"Crystal will be waiting for you when we're done. Just text her before you leave. And oh, she says those assholes at the mine kicked them out of the parking lot. Do you know of another place where you can meet to shoot your stand-up? Some place with a good backdrop?"

Leah's heart sank. Another unfamiliar term. "My stand-up?"

Rhonda groaned. "Sorry, yeah. You know, where the reporter stands in front of the camera for a few seconds, just talking about an aspect of the story. It's usually used at the beginning and when there's no video to show whatever the reporter is talking about. I can't believe we're doing this!"

"I can't either," Leah said. "And yes, I do know a spot. There's a turnout on the road leading to the mine. It has a great view of the whole operation, with the mountains in the background. I can meet her there." After they hung up, Leah texted Crystal to confirm their meeting time—ten o'clock—and gave her directions on how to find the location.

After kissing Harper good morning and explaining the situation to her mother, who clapped her hands in delight at the news, Leah poured herself a mug of coffee and went to work. When she was satisfied with what she'd written, she realized she hadn't checked the Mine Safety and Health Administration's website to see if they'd uploaded a fatality report. It might contain some new, useful information.

Leah did a quick search. There was a report, but it was too early for details. It had the incident's classification—Slip or Fall of Person—and that it occurred underground. No name. No conclusions.

The mine company had posted a brief news release about the accident, but it seemed intended to confirm the first day of operations would continue as scheduled. It would be helpful to know if they planned to release any more information before she wrote her story. Leah dialed the number she had for Morgan, and a man answered.

"No, we don't foresee any updates on the accident today," he said, then hung up.

Writing the TV script was easier than she'd imagined. Much easier. When she was done, she read the script aloud, made a few tweaks to smooth out the flow, then emailed it.

Ten minutes later, sipping her second cup of coffee, she received a reply.

OMG! THIS IS AMAZING. YOU NAILED IT. SENDING EDITED SCRIPT BACK NOW.

When she opened the document, she saw with surprise Rhonda had made few changes, and she flopped back in her chair, relieved.

Invigorated by the new challenge, Leah scurried to the bathroom and put on her makeup with extra care. She cursed as she rummaged through the closet. Leah hadn't brought much with her that would work on camera. What did reporters wear, anyway? After watching several videos on her computer, she decided a purple blouse and her best pair of high-waisted jeans should work. She was, after all, covering the opening of a mine. If Randall King could wear them on the air, so could she.

Leah was driving toward the Prestwich Tunnel, singing along to Britney Spears's "Work Bitch" on the radio, when she remembered Daniel. The young photographer was lying in a morgue, while she was happily contemplating her future.

The time on the dash read 9:20 a.m. Even with a ten-minute wait for the outbound traffic to clear the tunnel, she'd have plenty of time to get to her appointment with Crystal.

She turned the radio back on and settled in to listen to the public radio station. They were doing a whole hour on wealthy people moving into Jackson Hole with all-cash offers, driving home prices sky high. An interesting enough program to keep her mind off Mig and the mystery of the copper nugget.

Which reminded her.

Leah reached into her pocket and, opening the window, tossed the copper nugget onto the road. It bounced a few times, then rolled out of view.

Good riddance.

Driving through the tunnel was slow going. It often happened that way, when the first person through was a first-timer and the narrowness caught them off guard. Being forced to drive so slowly was irritating, but it was also easier. All she had to do was give the car in front of her plenty of space and follow the taillights. The driver made it easy, keeping a steady pace, instead of doing that thing that annoyed the hell out of Leah—speeding up, then slamming on the brakes every few yards. She was last in line, so at least she didn't have to worry about getting rear-ended.

When she reached the spot where Morgan had suffered her panic attack and had stopped her car, Leah's thoughts returned to that day. It was only three days ago, but with everything that had happened, it seemed like a week. She'd passed the point where Harper had waved to someone on the pedestrian walkway and where Morgan said she'd seen a shadow.

Leah squinted at the path. The yellow lights didn't quite reach where the walkway met the tunnel wall. It was dark and easy to imagine shadows lurking there. She forced her eyes back to the road where they belonged. If she drifted any further to the left, she'd scrape the wall. It was so close, if she lowered the window, she could reach out and touch it.

Finally, she glimpsed brilliant blue ahead. Another gorgeous day in Wyoming. It wouldn't be long before she was out of the gloomy confines of the Prestwich Squeeze and back on the open road. The car ahead honked several times as it exited the tunnel.

Startled, Leah flinched.

When her eyes popped back open, she saw a flash of color.

The Blazer shuddered. Something rolled on the hood, then slammed into the windshield—a yellow whip of color. A face mashed against the glass, eyes bulging. Leah's foot hit the brake. She had the fleeting impression of a mannequin before it rolled off the hood.

Stunned, Leah sat clutching the steering wheel, breathing raggedly. Someone was knocking on the window.

"Are you okay?" a voice called.

And then a scream. Followed by another.

Leah clawed at the door handle. When she finally managed to open it, she stumbled out and nearly fell.

Several people were crowded around a figure on the ground. A broken body with a smashed face, covered in blood.

It was Morgan. The young woman who'd lost her job at the mine. The young woman she'd helped through the tunnel just a few days before.

Chapter 13

The sheriff's deputy asked the small crowd a series of questions. No one could answer, except for Leah. All her muscles had gone numb, including those in her throat. She had to clear it several times before the words came out, and when they did, she hardly recognized the hoarse voice as her own.

Yes, she knew who it was. Morgan Bryne, the new director of communications for the mine. Would the young woman have any reason to end her life? Possibly. She'd lost her job. Leah refused to share any details in front of the crowd of strangers but instead gave the officer Mig's contact information. Had anyone seen Morgan with another person before the incident or earlier in the day? No, but Leah was able to offer at least one valuable bit of information.

As sirens wailed in the distance, she pointed to the hill directly above the tunnel.

"There's a path up there. It starts in town and connects to another one in the Dinky Minors. It's a hiking trail now, but before cars, people rode their horses up there. Maybe Morgan was taking a walk, clearing her head. The path gets narrow above the entrance to the Squeeze, so maybe she tripped and fell?"

Morgan discovering the trail after one day in town made that scenario unlikely, but Leah didn't mention that.

Eventually, more sheriff's officers arrived and then an ambulance. Leah watched, slightly dizzy, as two paramedics loaded Morgan's ruined body onto a gurney. She jumped when the doors slammed. Such a final, heartbreaking sound.

After she'd given her statement, the officer looked at her with concern. "Are you okay to drive?"

Leah nodded, remembering the sound of the young woman's body thudding against the metal hood. The phone chimed in her pocket. Pulling it out, she saw she'd missed a string of texts from Crystal, wondering where she was.

Jesus. Not only was she late, but she'd also nearly forgotten about the appointment to shoot the TV story. She tapped out a message to Crystal, who immediately responded: WTF?!!!

Both windshield wipers were busted, and the glass and hood of the car were smeared with blood. Leah's stomach heaved as she surveyed the gruesome aftermath of Morgan's fall. While it was revolting to behold, the Blazer hadn't sustained enough damage to prevent her from driving. Wyoming drivers were a hardy bunch. If anyone spotted blood on the truck, they'd assume she'd hit a deer. It happened all the time.

She was climbing into the car, when one of the officers returned carrying a large container of water.

"Close the door and let's see how much we can get off."

Squeezing her eyes shut as the water hit the red streaks, she waited until he knocked on the window. He produced a rag and wiped down the windshield, then gave her a friendly wave.

Leah was in no mood to work, but there was no getting out of it. And it could just be the distraction she needed to get through the next few hours. The sheriffs had closed off both entrances to the tunnel to investigate Morgan's death, so there was no returning home without driving an extra fifteen miles. Besides, she'd never missed a deadline.

On the short drive to meet Crystal, her thoughts went to Morgan. On the tour, she'd seemed in control. Not at all like the fragile woman Leah encountered having a panic attack. But then she'd lost her job. Mig said she'd taken it badly and had to be driven home.

But what had happened, exactly? Had Morgan been walking along the hill trail and fallen? Or had she made her way down from the trail to the tunnel opening and thrown herself into the path of the outbound cars? It was an odd place, and an odd way, to take one's life. It also required planning and effort. The hill above the tunnel was steep and treacherous. Leah hadn't noticed what kind of shoes Morgan had been wearing. Walking along the trail required nothing more than sneakers. Clambering down the hill to the tunnel was another matter. You'd need hiking boots with a good tread for that.

Neither scenario made any sense. Morgan, in her carefully matched work outfit, didn't seem the hiking type. If Leah had to guess, Morgan was more likely to binge-watch rom coms than go for a brisk walk.

She could guess all she wanted and still be no closer to the truth. The sheriff's office would investigate, and eventually, she'd learn what they determined.

Chapter 14

When Leah pulled up to the turnout above the mine, Crystal was waiting outside the satellite truck. Leah was surprised to see it. She didn't think the network would agree to loan it out to a competitor.

When she asked, Crystal said, "Oh, they don't own it. They just rent it out. In fact, they rent me out too. I work for a production company in Denver, so I drive this thing all over the place and do just about everything." Crystal paused, shaking her head at the Blazer and its badly dented hood. "Jesus. You could have been killed if she fell on the windshield. That's a weird way to off yourself, if you ask me." She paused. "Rhonda said this is your first time doing a package, and she wants me to field produce. That means I'll boss you around a little until we get the performance right. You okay with that?" The woman's short purple hair smelled of coconut shampoo. She wore a black "Bad Reputation" T-shirt with Joan Jett playing guitar, a jean jacket, and green pants. With her tight build and kohl-rimmed eyes, Crystal even resembled Joan Jett.

"Of course," Leah said. "I have no idea what I'm doing, so I'm counting on you to make sure I don't make a fool of myself on national television."

Crystal grinned, revealing a row of perfect white teeth. "I've got your back. You want to show me your script?"

They spent the next ten minutes in the satellite truck—Leah speaking into a microphone, reading her news story, starting and stopping along the way, following Crystal's coaching.

When they were done, Crystal said, "Wow, are you sure that's your first time? Randall King still pops his 'Ps'. Okay, let's go do your stand-up. You need more eyeliner. *Way* more. You gotta do the whole smoky-eye thing."

Leah pulled her makeup kit out of her tote bag and made the adjustments.

"Too much?" she asked when she was done.

Crystal leaned against a counter, studying her. "Not for the camera."

They went outside. Thankfully, there was no wind, and the sky was clear, except for a few long, wispy clouds. Leah's limbs no longer felt like jelly, and the fog had left her brain. Grateful for the distraction of work, she stood where Crystal pointed, standing a few yards from the edge of the turnout, with her back to the bustling mine. The insistent beeping of a truck reversing drifted up from below.

"Great location, by the way," Crystal called, one eye pressed against the viewfinder. "Can you scoot a little to your right? Great. That's it."

Leah complied, clenching her fists. "Do I look like a giant?"

Crystal straightened. "What do you mean?"

Leah made a sweeping gesture, starting from the top of her head, downward. "My size. The camera makes everything look bigger."

"Don't be ridiculous," Crystal scoffed. "You might be taller than Randall King, but you're hotter."

Leah's mouth had gone completely dry. Her skin itched. "I don't think I can do this."

"Of course, you can do this," Crystal snapped. "What's wrong with you?"

"*I'm* what's wrong with me," Leah said, pacing. "I can't. I just can't. I've never done this before. Someone at the network is going to see this, and they're going to say, 'oh my God, we had no idea she was so big.' Rhonda's never seen me in person. She's going to freak out."

Crystal scowled, hands on her hips. "The only one who's freaking out is you. You need to get over yourself. Rhonda is expecting a package."

Leah rubbed her sweaty palms on her jeans. "Can't we do it without the stand-up? Just this once?"

"You might not get a second chance," Crystal said. "Rhonda's nice, but she doesn't mess around." She stared up at the sky for a moment, blinking. "Okay. Tell her you were too upset after the accident, and you couldn't pull it together. But then you need to figure this shit out. Rhonda said she wants you as a reporter, but that's not going to happen until you can do a stand-up, like everyone else."

Leah nodded, blinking back unexpected tears. "Yeah, okay. Of course. Thank you."

Inside the satellite truck, Leah called and explained the situation to Rhonda, while Crystal listened, arms folded across her chest. Rhonda wasn't nearly as sympathetic as Leah expected.

"Are you sure?" Rhonda said. "I already told the executive producer about the story. It was going to be your audition. If he liked it, you're in."

Leah swallowed. "I'm really sorry, but I can't."

"All right. But you better knock it out of the park next time to make up for this."

Rhonda spoke loud enough for Crystal to hear every word. When they'd disconnected, Crystal said, "At least she'll give you another shot."

Leah collapsed into a chair, suddenly exhausted. Failing to perform on the job was a new experience. She prided herself on delivering news stories that were impeccably researched, well-written, and on deadline. But now, she was being asked to do something outside of her comfort zone, and it was unpleasant as hell. She might have jeopardized a fantastic opportunity, one that could translate into a lot more money. And she wasn't getting any younger. Some would argue she was already too old to make the leap to TV, and she'd just wimped out on the one chance she'd been given.

Leah was being ridiculous. But she was also scared. Scared of what might happen on social media and the derision she might face for her size, which even seemed to be an issue for her own mother.

Crystal punched her in the arm. "Hey, it's just fucking TV, and we still have work to do."

Biting her lip, Leah studied the script on her phone. "What do we do without the stand-up?"

Crystal slid the mic across the counter. "Record what you were going to say. We'll have to use more pool video to cover it. It's not ideal, but we can make it work."

When she'd finished tracking, Leah said, "When you sent the pool video out, did you include the part with Daniel's accident?"

Crystal kept her eyes on the screen. "Hell no. And Randall didn't want to include that weird shit on the wall, the 'curse this place' stuff. He wanted to hang onto it, just in case it turned out to be a big deal, so his network would have an exclusive."

"Can they do that?"

"A normal news operation wouldn't," Crystal said with a shrug, "but these guys don't always play by the rules. There's nothing I can do about it. I'm just a worker bee."

"Can I see it?"

Crystal's hands froze above the keyboard. Her mouth twitched. "Yeah," she finally said. "But only because you don't have a stick up your butt, like most people I work with. I'll copy the whole thing off on a thumb drive, but you've got to promise me you're not going to use it. If I find out you do, you'll have made an enemy of me forever, and man, I win awards for holding a grudge. You cool with that?"

"Totally cool."

When Crystal was done, they watched the two-minute story from start to finish, Leah sitting up a little straighter toward the end. She might not have appeared on camera, but she sounded good, confident.

"Nice work," Crystal said. "It would have been better if you weren't such a chickenshit and did the stand-up."

Leah exhaled loudly. "Thank you. I have no idea how you did that, but you're a miracle worker."

"Teamwork," Crystal said, bumping her fist.

When she'd finished uploading the file, Leah texted Rhonda they'd sent it off, then settled in to wait for feedback.

Crystal swiveled in her chair to face her. "Did I hear right? That you're from Tribulation Gulch? We're booked into the hotel on the main street. It's like being on a Western movie set or something. What was it like growing up in such a small town?" Her green eyes glowed with curiosity.

"Challenging," Leah said. Living in Tribulation Gulch meant being the twin sister of a murdered child. But she wasn't about to talk about that.

Crystal drummed her black fingernails on the counter. "Challenging? That's it? That's all I get?"

Leah sighed. "It's pretty much how you'd imagine. Everybody knows everybody…and their business. After the mine shut down and people started moving away, the place got a little smaller. And sadder. The mine reopening is a big deal, as you can imagine. It's just getting started, but downtown looks like a whole new place."

Crystal gave a thoughtful nod, then her eyes popped open, and she snapped her fingers. "I know what I wanted to ask you! Have you heard about that new true crime documentary? The one about the guy who killed some kids back in the eighties?" She rolled her chair to a mini fridge, rummaged inside, and handed Leah a bottle of water. "That was here, right? I'm not mixing it up with some other place in Wyoming?"

The plastic bottle slipped from Leah's fingers. "It was here, all right," she said, bending to pick up the bottle. "I was just a kid when it happened. I haven't seen the documentary, but I heard about it. To tell you the truth, I hate true crime stuff. It's a little too creepy for me."

Which was the truth. She hated shows about serial killers, and it seemed there was no escaping them these days. Cheap to produce, with just enough truth to feel legit. And built-in viewership—some people couldn't get enough of that kind of thing, and the grislier the better.

But Leah wasn't an average viewer. Her brother had been the victim of a serial killer, and it could just as easily have been her that day, thirty-five years ago.

The producer of *The Copper Man: The Story of George Cunliffe* had tracked Leah down and asked for an interview, promising to go about it with great sensitivity. Leah doubted that. Before she'd returned his call, she'd sampled his true crime shows and found them sensational and exploitative. She'd declined, offering no explanations.

The next day, her mother called, upset, saying "some jackass from Hollywood" was harassing her, trying to get her to talk about Liam. So much for sensitivity.

"Well, it's out today, if you're curious," Crystal said. "I know I'm going to watch it. I'm staying in town another night, and I've got nothing better to do."

Leah was more than curious. Now that she knew it existed, she wouldn't be able to stop thinking about it until she saw it.

Chapter 15

"You look wrung out, Leah. First that young man yesterday, and now this. Everyone is talking about it," Leah's mother fretted as she cleared the dinner dishes. "Why don't you go on upstairs and take a nice hot bath or something."

A bath sounded nice, but Leah had something else in mind. She went to her room, hopped in bed, put in her ear buds, and searched for The Copper Man documentary on her laptop.

There were two episodes. The idea of watching both made her reach for the wine glass on the nightstand.

Downstairs, her mother and Harper moved around the living room. The fairy kingdom had outgrown the coffee table, and her mother had brought up boxes from the basement, draping them in green felt.

"I think we need a lake, Gimme," Leah heard Harper call.

At its current rate of expansion, the fairy kingdom would take over the entire living room before they left.

Leah forced her attention back to the laptop and tapped play.

The first ten minutes introduced viewers to the town of Tribulation Gulch and the horrific crimes committed in 1985.

The faceless narrator, a man, introduced the victims, ranging in age from five to eleven. Two girls and three boys, all children of mine company executives who lived in

Tribulation Gulch. None of the victims' families had given interviews, but a handful of locals had agreed to talk on camera. They seemed to relish the telling, recalling the town's shock at the children's disappearances, then later, the discovery of their bloodied bodies, each with a copper nugget tucked in a pocket.

There was video of the large, well-kept houses where the children had lived, the elementary school, and aerial shots highlighting the isolation of the area and the rugged terrain. Without much else to say about the victims, the documentary shifted to the killer.

"*George Cunliffe was born in Fergus County, Montana, where his parents operated a large, prosperous cattle ranch. But the life of a cowboy wasn't for George, who preferred collecting rocks and minerals to riding horses and herding cattle. Against his family's wishes, he went to Montana Technological University, where he earned a degree in metallurgical engineering. Eventually, he was to take a job at the Prestwich Copper Mine in Tribulation Gulch.*"

For this part of the documentary, the producers had little material to work with: a few shots of the small campus, and two photos of George Cunliffe as a college student.

Leah bent over the screen, heart beating faster. He was younger than the man she remembered from that day in 1985. More dark hair on the top of his head. Not bad-looking, but also nondescript. His nose veered slightly left, but it was hardly distinctive. His eyes were dark and rather intense, but that was just his expression.

Not much was known about his personal life after he moved to Tribulation Gulch. He took a job at the mine as a metallurgist, met a secretary, and they married. There was no wedding photo, just a copy of the marriage certificate followed by several photos of his wife, a pretty woman with a mass of dark hair.

At some point, the couple moved to a large property outside of town, near the Dinky Minor hills. Video showed an isolated home gone to ruin, surrounded by sagging fences.

"*What we do know,*" the narrator said, "*is that George Cunliffe had become disillusioned with his work at the mine and wanted to return to his roots. He inherited enough money to purchase this piece of land, where he started a cattle ranch. But things began to happen that were beyond his control. An accident at the mine sent polluted runoff into the groundwater Cunliffe relied on for his ranch. The water coming from Cunliffe's well became too toxic for his family or his livestock to drink.*

"*Cunliffe threatened to sue the mine, but then something mysterious happened instead. Inexplicably, he returned to his old job at the mine but with a better title and higher salary. Nobody knows exactly what brought Cunliffe back. Did the company admit their negligence had ruined his property? Did they buy his silence?*

"*What we do know is, Cunliffe returned to work bitter and angry. Co-workers said only two things in his life brought him joy: his wife and his son.*"

Leah gasped and paused the video. She knew Cunliffe had been married but not that he'd been a father.

How could she have not known such an important detail? She'd never made any special effort looking into his history. Leah, who made her living digging up information for a living, had left Cunliffe's life story dead and buried. But she'd have thought the gossip at the time would have included that bit of news.

"*Cunliffe, already reeling from the devaluation of his property, was soon to receive another blow. His wife, at the age of thirty-eight, was diagnosed with advanced breast cancer, and within a year, she was dead.*

Then his son, just five years old, began having serious health challenges of his own. He became a brittle asthmatic and frequently required an inhaler to breathe.

"Those who knew him say Cunliffe blamed pollution from the mine for all his troubles: the poisoning of his water supply, the toxins in the air he believed caused his wife's cancer, the lethal dust he was convinced caused his son's asthma.

"And as bad as things were for George Cunliffe, things were about to get much, much worse."

That ended the first episode.

Leah fell back against the pillows. How could a father of a young child go on to kill other children? She drained the rest of her wine and hit play on the second episode.

What she heard next brought tears to her eyes. Little Michael Cunliffe's asthma worsened. Despite heavy doses of steroids, his attacks became increasingly severe.

The photos showed an adorable child with wispy dark hair.

The narrator continued. *"One afternoon, Michael Cunliffe suffered an asthma attack while playing outside his home. The attack was so severe, he died before medical help could arrive.*

"Several of Cunliffe's colleagues, who declined to appear on camera, told us he had long taken issue with the mine's impact on the environment, including risks to public health. They believe Cunliffe came to blame the mine's executives for the death of his wife and only son."

Leah hit pause with a trembling finger. Over the years, she'd never given much thought to The Copper Man's motivation for killing five children.

Revenge.

Cunliffe killed the children to get back at the people he blamed for his son's death.

116

Leah's father had been a lead project engineer. His work touched on all aspects of the mining operation. It was no mystery why Cunliffe had made him a target.

There were only forty minutes left. She might as well finish it. If she didn't, she'd wonder what she'd missed and lose sleep over it. She continued playing the video.

The documentary switched gears, introducing someone who'd not yet appeared—a detective from the sheriff's office assigned to the case, now retired.

A vague memory flickered. Then, she remembered—recognized him. He'd visited her house, sat across from her in the living room, and asked questions in a quiet voice. Leah couldn't recall what he asked, but she could remember his manner. Kind. Patient.

But there had been tension in the room. The air had practically crackled with it. Her mother sobbing, her father pacing. It was all coming back in a rush. The officer had driven her home in the back of his car. People had come running after they'd heard her terrified screams behind a barn at the rodeo carnival grounds. Then she remembered watching The Copper Man carry off her brother.

The man she was looking at on the screen had held her by the hand and led her into her house to safety.

The retired officer's name was Mark Schulze. He was explaining how, despite the manpower devoted to investigating the murders, they'd failed to identify a suspect.

George Cunliffe had managed to abduct and kill five children without attracting any attention.

He'd been a law-abiding citizen. The only clue he'd left behind were the copper nuggets in the pockets of his victims, and those were sold all over town as souvenirs. It was only after he'd thrown himself off the Prestwich Bridge that they'd discovered his truck and the evidence left behind. Lengths of rope. Bloodied hunting knives. A box of latex gloves. A pink sandal belonging to one of the victims.

Unlike other serial killers, George Cunliffe did not dismember the bodies, torture his victims, nor sexually assault them. He stabbed them once through the throat and disposed of them in the hills above town. All except for Liam, whose body was found in the same tailings pond where Cunliffe's body had fallen from the old trestle above.

Schulze stared straight into the camera. "*We thought the manner of death was significant. Of course, we'll never know for sure, but Cunliffe's son died because he had an asthma attack and couldn't breathe. Cunliffe was out for revenge. He wanted to get back at the people he held responsible for the death of his son by slashing the throats of their children.*" A long silence followed.

The camera zoomed into Schulze's weather-worn face.

A voice off camera said, "*Mr. Schulze, we heard there was a video of one of the abductions. Of five-year-old Liam Shaw being kidnapped at the rodeo carnival.*"

Leah's heart slammed against her chest. Without taking her eyes off the screen, she turned up the audio.

She watched Schulze shift in his chair. He cleared his throat, then gave a curt nod. "*We heard that too.*"

"*But did you see it?*" pressed the off-camera voice. "*For yourself?*"

"*If such a video existed, it was never entered into evidence,*" Schulze replied.

"*But did you see it?*"

Schulze hesitated. "*No. That rumor got started because some people at the rodeo saw a TV reporter covering the event. For some reason,*" *they thought he filmed the abduction. I talked to the reporter myself, a man named Bill Kimball. He said he neither witnessed nor filmed the abduction, so I have to believe him."*

He's lying, Leah thought. When the documentary ended, she did a search for Bill Kimball. He'd retired and was now teaching broadcast journalism in Logan, Utah. His webpage listed his contact information, which she added to her phone.

Leah lay awake, thinking about Bill Kimball. If there was any chance the former TV reporter caught Liam's abduction on video, she had to talk to him.

There was something off about that day, thirty-five years ago.

She'd only been five at the time, but she had always sensed she didn't have the full story. Something important lingered in the shadows of her memory. If there was a video, maybe the answer was there.

Over the years, a succession of therapists had reassured Leah it was perfectly normal to remember some things and not others, given her age and the trauma of the event. She recalled the way the man seemed to appear out of nowhere, the way his eyes narrowed and his face twisted, the way she knew he was the bad man everyone was talking about.

The part that came after George Cunliffe first showed up but before he carried off Liam was gone from her memory.

If she could explain that to Bill Kimball, if he did have the video, maybe he would understand and show it to her. What reason did he have to lie, to say the video didn't exist? What would make him claim he hadn't shot it in the first place?

Chapter 16

Patricia had taken Harper to a Story Time event at the library, so Leah was on her own. She had plenty of work to keep her busy, like writing a piece on the economic comeback of Tribulation Gulch, but working out of the big, quiet house alone held little appeal. What she needed was some background noise, and maybe even a glass of wine.

Of the two saloons in Tribulation Gulch, she chose Boxcar Willy's because the other was crowded with tourists staying in town after a day on the river.

Willy's was the local's favorite. The interior hadn't been touched in decades, and if Willy the Third ever decided to do a little upgrade, he'd get an earful from the regulars.

A few men sat drinking and smoking at the bar. They were too busy talking to notice new arrivals, and that was fine by Leah. A dog came to greet her, and she bent over to scratch its head.

A bearded man in a flannel shirt, jean jacket, and cowboy hat waved from a bar stool. "Jackson's fine. He doesn't bite."

A little late for that, Leah thought, her face inches from the dog's muzzle. A shepherd of some sort, it's shiny coat cleaner than the man's pants—he looked like he'd spent the day mucking out a barn.

No one could call Boxcar Willy's a tourist trap, not with its mismatched chairs, worn linoleum, and dusty antlers hanging from the wood-paneled walls. At the back end, there was a pool table and three dart boards, although no one was playing. It was too early for that. At night, Boxcar Willy's transformed into a raucous place, where mine workers gathered to gossip and occasionally get into fights.

At the bar, Leah asked for a glass of white wine, and the bartender, a plump woman in her seventies, surprised her by asking, "And what kind would you like? We've got chardonnay, sauvignon blanc, and some real nice pinot grigio."

"That pinot grigio's pretty good," Jackson's owner said. "It's what my wife has, when I can get her to join me."

"She'd join you more if you washed off the barn before you came in." The bartender laughed.

Jackson's owner drained the last of his beer and slid the empty glass across the counter. "Well, you got a point there because that's what she says. Trouble is, after I'm done here, taking a little break, I got a few more hours of work to do. There's no rest for the wicked." He turned in his chair to face Leah, one elbow propped on the counter. "You aren't Patricia Shaw's girl, are you?"

Leah nodded, surprised. She didn't resemble her mother, so it wasn't something that usually occurred to people. Which meant he knew who she was, and he meant to start a conversation.

"I am," she admitted.

"How about that," the man said, then leaned over to scratch behind Jackson's ears.

A cryptic response, if there ever was one. Leah accepted her glass of chilled wine and found a table near the front window where she could look out on the street, a safe distance from the bar.

The wine was delicious. Dry and crisp. She slipped her laptop out of her tote bag and fired it up. Within minutes, she was writing. When she glanced up, the man with the dog was leaning over the counter, having a whispered conversation with the bartender. Leah briefly wondered what all that was about, then turned her attention to the screen. She'd finished nearly five hundred words, when she felt someone standing over her.

"Mind if I join you?" Mr. Dirty Pants asked. He was holding a full pint of beer.

As much as she wanted to say no, that she was busy working, she didn't want to be rude, and she didn't get the sense he was hitting on her.

"Have a seat," she said, sounding sharper than she intended.

The man didn't seem to notice. He sat, the dog flopping down at his feet with a contented sigh. "I'm Randy Laybourn, and you're probably wondering why I'm pestering you. Well. I'll tell you. I knew your father, way back from our Kennecott days in Utah. He was the main reason I ended up here. He helped get me a job."

"He did?" she asked, unable to keep the surprise out of her face. Leah knew most of her parents' acquaintances in town.

"He sure did. I'm a geologist. Retired now. I bought a small ranch to keep myself busy. Got a bit more than I bargained for."

Randy had an impressive handlebar mustache, faded brown at the top, silver on the bottom. He seemed to be mulling over what to say next. Leah braced herself. Over the course of her career as a journalist, she'd done enough interviews to know that look. The look of someone choosing their words carefully.

"That's nice," she said.

Randy grabbed a napkin from a holder on the table and mopped his beard. "If my wife were here, she'd tell me to keep my mouth shut, but since she's not, I just wanted to let you know how your father used to talk about you all the time. He used to say how smart you were, and brave too. He was so excited when you said you wanted to mutton bust. I saw you that day, you know. You held on tight and showed no fear." Randy shook his head. "It was awful the way that day turned out." He reached over and patted her hand. "But you know that, of course. I'm sorry for bringing it up."

Leah stared down at her empty glass. If she'd known the conversation was going to head in that direction, she'd have ordered a second.

"It's nice to hear that about my dad," she said.

And she meant it. She could only remember her father trying to cajole Liam into entering the mutton busting contest and making him cry. Her parents had argued over it, her record-breaking eleven-second ride overlooked.

"So, you knew my parents in Utah?" she asked. Her mother rarely talked about their time there.

"That I did. We were good friends. In fact, I remember taking your dad out for a few drinks after they lost their firstborn. Never seen a man so gutted. And then they got you, and low and behold, there's your mother, expecting again. They just couldn't believe it."

Leah blinked. "Firstborn?"

Randy froze, glass mid-air.

"Are you saying my parents had a child? Before me and Liam?"

Randy set down his glass. His Adam's apple moved up and down as he swallowed. "They didn't tell you?"

"No," Leah said. "Never. How old was the baby?"

Another swallow. "A baby boy, if I remember right. Stillborn."

The sound of alarm bells going off in her head made it hard to think. She gave her head a little shake. "What did you mean when you said, they *got* me? You said they *got* me, and then my mother was expecting?"

The parts of Randy's face not blanketed in facial hair paled. "I've really put my foot in it, haven't I?"

Leah sat very straight in her chair and folded her hands on the table. "You're going to have to spell this out for me, Randy, because right now, I'm very, very confused."

He stared at her for a long time, then took a swig of beer. "All right, then. Seeing as you don't seem to know...And if that's the case, then you surely deserve to. After they lost their first baby, your dad said they wouldn't be able to have another. We had a few drinks over that bad news, let me tell you, and then one day, I was in Salt Lake, and I ran into them at ZCMI. And there you were, in a stroller. A brand new baby. Your dad said they'd just picked you up at an adoption agency."

Leah fell back in her chair. The muscles in her body had gone numb, but her mind raced.

Adopted. The man was telling her she was adopted.

This fact, this incredibly important fact, explained everything. Why she didn't look like her parents. Why, despite being twins, she and her brother had been nothing alike. And it explained something else. Her mother had fussed over Liam in a way she never had with Leah. She used to think it was because Liam was so small and sweet. Adorable. Loveable. Not like enormous Leah, with her long limbs and big hands. Her mother used to gaze at her hands during bath time and say, "Where in heaven's name did you get these things?"

Her confusion was turning to a rapidly boiling anger. She'd been lied to. Denied her history, her story.

Without a word, Randy got up, went to the bar, and a few moments later, returned with two small glasses. "Looks like you could do with a whiskey."

She eyed it gratefully and drank half of it, feeling the burn in her throat. It didn't come close to easing the knot of resentment coiling at the bottom of her stomach, but it took the edge off a bit.

"I'm sorry to have given you such a shock," Randy said.

Leah poked at the ice cubes in the glass with a skinny red straw. "I'm still confused. If I'm adopted, why did my parents say I was Liam's twin?"

Randy shook his head. "Now, that I can't tell you. What I can tell you is that your mom was, pardon the expression, ready to pop when I saw her out shopping at ZCMI. I'm pretty sure she had your brother just a few days after that. In fact, I know that's right because your dad and I were supposed to have lunch together, and he called me to say Patricia had gone into labor, so he couldn't make it."

Leah tugged her upper lip a few times. "Just curious. Who else around town knows I'm adopted?"

Randy's bushy eyebrows shot up. "A lot of us older people, I should think." He jerked his head in the direction of the bartender. "Marcy knows. My wife too, of course. You know. People talk."

Not to me, Leah thought bitterly.

She drained the rest of her whiskey. With trembling fingers that felt like they weren't attached to her body, she gathered her things, thanked Randy for the bombshell, then crossed the bar toward the exit. At the door, she turned and gave him a little wave to show she harbored no ill feelings.

The man looked miserable. He gave a sheepish wave in return.

Two drinks didn't mix well with the shock she'd just received. She was having an out-of-body experience. Before she went home, she needed a few moments to think. Leah drove slowly down Center Street, then meandered through the neighborhoods. The afternoon had turned cloudy, blotting out the sun.

Her parents had told everyone she and Liam were twins. Not something they could do in Utah, where everyone knew them, but easy when they moved to Tribulation Gulch just after her first birthday. That's when the fiction had started.

But why? Why resort to such a ridiculous and elaborate lie?

It was a question only her mother could answer.

Chapter 17

Leah waited until Harper was asleep before confronting her mother. Getting through dinner and her daughter's bedtime routine had been a challenge, an endless stream of questions bubbling up in her head as the evening wore on.

Harper had sensed her distraction while they snuggled together, reading *Fantastic Mr. Fox.*

"Mom, you're not saying it right," Harper said. A small finger landed accusingly on a paragraph.

Leah frowned at the words. "Yes, I am."

Harper pointed again, this time at the word "where" in italics. "That's the part you didn't say right."

Leah had scooped Harper onto her lap and given her a squeeze. "There's no fooling you, kiddo. You're correct. I didn't read it right. I made it sound all boring."

Harper patted the side of her face. "That's okay, Mom. Gimme says you're working very hard, and we should be extra nice to you."

Leah had stiffened. She hadn't yet considered how Harper might be impacted by her status as an adoptee. For one, it meant Harper wasn't biologically related to her beloved Gimme. For another, it meant Harper had a right to that information too, but when? When was the right time to tell a child something like that? Harper was smart. Once told, she'd begin to wonder about the other woman who was also her grandmother, and her grandfather too.

Leah had forced her attention back to the adventures of Mr. Fox, read another two chapters in a bright, enthusiastic voice, then tucked Harper in.

"Gimme says we're going to Shelley's tomorrow so I can play with Mason and Sofia," Harper said, clutching Chicken to her chest.

"That sounds like fun."

Which had reminded Leah to text Mig. He'd sent another message while she was giving Harper a bath, trying to lock down their dinner date. In the hall, she tapped back that things were weird at home, and she'd get back to him as soon as she could.

He had replied immediately. *How weird?*

Really weird. I'll tell you later.

Tease.

Flirty, she thought as she went downstairs.

At the sight of her mother reading, feet propped up on an upholstered ottoman, Mig disappeared from her thoughts. She fell into the easy chair opposite.

"Did my granddaughter make you read an entire novel?" Patricia asked. She was still reading the Margaret Thatcher biography.

"Almost," Leah said, voice icy.

The book lowered. Her mother stared at her over the top of her reading glasses. "Rough bedtime?"

Now that the time had arrived, Leah had no idea how to start the conversation. Which thread to pull first to unravel this giant mess of deception? A trickle of sweat ran down her back. "We need to talk."

"Oh?" Her mother set aside the book with a sigh. She folded her hands and placed them on her lap. "And what would you like to talk about?" Patricia was using the same voice she reserved for difficult clients.

Leah's pulse pounded in her veins. Her throat tightened, and she had to swallow a few times to loosen the words stuck in her throat. "My adoption."

Her mother's eyebrows shot up. "Who told you?"

Leah wasn't sure what she was expecting, but it wasn't that cool, brisk response.

"A man named Randy Laybourn. I ran into him in town, and we got to talking." Tears welled in her eyes. She wiped them away with the back of her hand. "Mom, how could you not tell me? Why did you…lie?"

Patricia frowned. "It was a decision we made to protect you, and Randy had no right to talk about things that are none of his business. But that's Randy for you. He and your father were friends, but I never liked the man, and when they followed us here, I refused to have anything to do with them."

"Because they knew your secret," Leah cried. "Tell me more about that, Mom. The truth, my history, everything you've been keeping from me!"

"Honestly, Leah, you're being overly dramatic about this," her mother snapped. "We intended to tell you, eventually. But then Liam"—she paused—"died, and then how could we? You'd lost your brother in the most terrible way possible, and it took years for you to get over your night terrors."

Leah was shaking her head. "No. You did it for *you*. Not me. What was it? Shame? Didn't want anyone to think our little family wasn't perfect?"

"That's ridiculous. Just listen to yourself. You became a different child after that. Clingy and needy. How could we tell you? That was another shock you didn't need. We made that decision because we thought it was in your best interest. It wasn't about us. It was about you. You became such an insecure child, and then an insecure teenager, that to tell you something like that seemed cruel."

"Not telling me was wrong," Leah exploded. "I had a right to know. That's my history. My identity."

Her mother winced. "You have an identity, Leah Shaw, one we have given you, along with everything else over the years. Did you not have a loving, good, stable home? Did I not send you to the college of your choice, all expenses paid? Have I not helped you, financially, when you needed it? And look at you now. Soon to be a reporter on national television. I'd say we'd made the right decision. Who knows how things would have turned out if we told you and you hadn't reacted well? Gone into a depression, or who knows what!"

Leah leapt to her feet and began pacing. "I can't believe this. You're not the least bit sorry.

"Why should I be?" her mother sniffed. "I haven't done anything wrong."

Leah stopped and glared at her. "I'm pretty sure, if I talked to a psychologist, they'd disagree." A moan of frustration escaped her lips. "I thought I was a twin, for God's sake. Do you have any idea how I'm feeling right now?"

"Yes, like you're incapable of seeing my point of view. I think we should continue this conversation later, when you're able to be rational."

"You're kidding?"

"No. No, I'm not kidding. And with that, I'm going to bed. Goodnight." Her mother snatched up her book and swept from the room.

Leah stared at the ceiling, fighting back tears, hands balled into fists.

Chapter 18

Leah's mother didn't apologize—that wasn't her style—but she did act conciliatory the next morning. "I know you're upset, dear, and we'll talk about this again, but I just hope you can see it in your heart to give your mother a break, after all she's been through."

If Harper hadn't been in the next room, Leah might have lost it, then and there. That her mother had addressed herself in third person, like the queen, suggested she'd distanced herself from her actions. It was obvious her mother wasn't going to take responsibility for keeping the adoption a secret. Then playing the pity card! As if she'd been the only one traumatized by Liam's murder. It was enough to make Leah's body thrum with fury.

"I am upset, Mom," she said, snatching a slice of bread from the toaster. She wagged a knife in her direction. "And you're damn right we'll talk about this again. I still have lots of questions. Like what you know about my birth family."

Patricia was dressed in designer jeans and a blue sweatshirt. She was taking Harper to Shelley's for a playdate with Mig's children. Glancing up from her breakfast of yogurt and blueberries, Patricia tapped her spoon on the edge of the bowl. "I'd be happy to tell you what little I know. I will say, before you get your hopes up, that woman preferred no contact."

Leah gripped the counter with both hands, jaw clenched so tight it hurt.

There it was. Out in the open for the first time—her mother's attitude about her birth mother.

That woman.

It took all of Leah's energy to resist shaking her mother by the shoulders and screaming, *Tell me everything you know, right now!*

But this was too enormous an issue to get into with Harper around, and they needed to get on with their day. Leah had two articles to write.

She finished her breakfast, then went into the living room to help Harper pack bits and pieces from her fairy kingdom to show her new friends.

"Can I bring this, Mom?" Harper asked, holding out her hand.

It was a copper nugget.

Leah's scalp prickled. She'd thrown what she thought was the only one in the house out the car window before entering the Prestwich Tunnel on the morning Morgan died. It was a new nugget. Where it came from, she couldn't imagine.

Leah shook her head. "Let's leave that here," she said, without explaining. "I think you're taking enough to Shelley's, don't you?" Without waiting for a reply, she snatched the nugget from Harper's hand, went into the kitchen, and dropped it into the trash can.

After her mother and Harper left, Leah went for a short run to clear her head, made a pot of coffee, and settled in at the kitchen to write on her laptop.

By four o'clock, there was no sign of her mother and Harper. They'd been gone all day. That had to be the longest playdate on record. At four thirty, Leah went into the front yard to stretch her legs. The lawn was wide and green, with a huge whitebark pine. She lifted her face to the sun, feeling its warmth against her skin.

Her cell phone rang. It was her mother.

"Is Harper okay?" Leah asked.

"Of course," her mother said briskly. "She's having a blast. In fact, Shelley and I came up with a little plan." There was a sly edge to her voice.

"Oh?"

"You said something about you and Mig getting together and catching up, and since the kids are making an entire fort, we thought if Mig got off work soon enough, you two could go out, and the rest of us will hang out together here and have dinner and watch movies. It'll be fun."

On playdates, Harper usually lasted two hours, max. If she had a meltdown, home was only a block away. The offer was too good to refuse, even from the woman who'd betrayed her with lies. A little extra time and space to process things might not be a bad idea, and she did want to see Mig alone, without the distraction of children.

"Are you sure?" Leah asked.

"I wouldn't have said it if I didn't mean it."

"Thank you," Leah said stiffly. "I'll tell Mig and see if this works for him."

"You're kidding?" Mig said after they'd placed their order. "And you never even suspected?"

Leah smiled at him across the table. They were sitting on the rear deck of The Greek Coffee Shop. It was early in the season to be dining outside, but a patio heater allowed them to enjoy the late spring air, and the string of lights made it cheerful. Since she'd last visited, the restaurant had begun serving dinner, and Mig swore the Greek chicken pot pie was the best thing he'd ever tasted.

"I never suspected a thing." Leah paused long enough to sip her wine. A good pinot noir. "But I was always confused about not looking like my parents, or my brother. Did your parents ever say anything?"

Mig picked up a basket, lifted the white cloth to reveal the pita bread, and held it across the table. She took it. It was so hot, she dropped it onto her plate.

"No, my folks never mentioned it." Mig paused. "What are you going to do?"

"There's not much I *can* do," Leah said slowly. "What's done is done, and my mother isn't one to apologize. She doesn't seem to think she's done anything wrong. And she's all I've got. Family-wise. Both my mom and my dad were only children, so it's not like I've got a bunch of cousins somewhere. And even though she drives me crazy, she's an amazing grandmother, and Harper adores her."

Mig dipped the corner of his pita into a shallow bowl of olive oil and rosemary. "No offense, but your mom is a piece of work."

"None taken," Leah said. "She is."

He leaned forward, resting his forearms on the table. Leah tried not to stare at his wrists. He had nice wrists. They were strangely sexy.

"Are you going to search for your birth parents?" he asked.

Leah tore off a piece of pita bread. "Definitely. I need to find out everything I can. Who they were. Why they decided

138

to give me up. My ancestry. Medical information. Whenever I went to the doctor, I just answered all those medical history questions as if I was biologically related to my mom and dad." She dragged her pita through the olive oil. "A few years ago, when I was the same age as my dad when he had his heart attack, I got nervous enough that I had some tests done." She paused. "I really need to calm down, sorry. I need to quit going on about this."

Mig reached over and squeezed her hand. "Leah, you get to talk about this as much as you want. This is a big deal."

She stared down at her hand covered by one larger than her own. A lump formed in her throat. "Thank you. I appreciate that."

Mig frowned slightly. "Wow. You sound so…formal."

"Maybe we should talk about something else. Have you heard anything about Morgan? Like, cause of death?"

Mig smiled, but it didn't quite reach his eyes. "Now you sound like a reporter, and I'm feeling a little exploited. If you really want to know, I'll tell you, but I didn't realize our dinner was going to be an 'on the record' kind of thing."

Leah held up her hands. "I'm sorry. Apparently, I've forgotten how to behave when I'm not working. Forget I even asked. Unless you want to tell me, then it's off the record. Also, in my defense, I met her on her first day in town, so I am curious."

"That's right." Mig nodded. "I forgot about that. I've not heard much, and it's not likely I will, unless the company was involved in some way. And I don't see how that's possible. There are only two options. You said it yourself. She either fell from the trail, or she jumped. But there is something I *can* tell you off the record…and this is just me venting after a few rough days at work, okay?"

"Let's hear it," Leah said. "You had to sit there and listen to my adoption drama."

Mig drained the last of his wine. "Since the photographer died, everyone working underground got even more nervous, talking about seeing things in the tunnels, or hearing voices. I think there's some serious pranking going on because we're suddenly having a graffiti problem. We get it painted over, and it's back again the next morning. We have security cameras, but we haven't caught anyone so far."

Their conversation was interrupted by the arrival of their server, Zoe, carrying their plates. Bechamel bubbled up around the edges of golden layers of phyllo dough. It tasted delicious. Savory, with a rich, creamy texture.

When Zoe returned to top off their glasses, Leah said, "Wow, these are amazing."

Zoe wore a black dress and bright green eyeshadow. "Totally. I'm, like, addicted. The secret ingredient is the feta. My grandma gets it from The Goat Man. I'm pretty sure he sells it to the public, if you want some."

"You mean, the old guy who lives in the hills at the end of town?" Mig asked.

"He's the one," Zoe said. "I forgot his name, but everyone calls him The Goat Man. He comes in a few times a week to deliver the cheese. My grandma says he used to be friends with—" Zoe clapped a hand over her mouth.

Leah glanced at Mig, who shrugged. "Used to be friends with who?" she asked.

Zoe grimaced. "Uh, I'm such an idiot. Here you are, trying to have a nice dinner and everything, except now, it'll be weird if I don't tell you. The Copper Man. My grandma says they used to be friends." Zoe mumbled her excuses and dashed off.

Mig speared a tomato on his plate. "So now we've got The Copper Man, The Goat Man, your mother gaslighting you, maybe a suicide, a fatal accident at the mine, and don't forget the 'I Curse This Place' messages showing up in the tunnels. Does that about sum it up?"

"You know where that message comes from, right?" Leah asked. "George Cunliffe's final words before he jumped off the Prestwich Bridge."

"So I heard," Mig said grimly. "Also, off the record, there's a theory going around that we've got an anti-mine activist employed underground, trying to shake things up. You know, scare the workers, cause some accidents. It seems a little far-fetched to me, but I don't know how else to explain everything that's going on."

The conversation moved on to their children, their failed marriages, and the status of their exes. Everything except the way their relationship had ended. No big breakup scene. They'd drifted apart in the first few months of college, and that had been that.

Leah had no intention of introducing the subject. It happened so long ago. Two decades of life lived apart. When she'd finished answering Mig's questions about how she came to be a journalist, he crumpled his napkin and dropped it onto his plate.

"I have an idea," he said. "Why don't you and Harper come over tomorrow for dinner? Just the five of us. I can fire up the grill, and we can do something easy. How does that sound?" When she didn't answer right away, he knocked his knee into hers under the table. "So there's no confusion, it's a date but with kids because we can't keep dumping them on other people."

"A date…," she said.

Mig smiled. "Technically, that's what this is, but I guess you didn't get the message. Is there a problem? We used to have a pretty good time."

That, exactly, was the problem. They used to have a wildly good time. But things were different now. More complicated. She had a kid. He had two. The kids got along and played together. And besides, what was the point? Mig lived in Wyoming. She lived in Colorado. People their age dated for two reasons: hoping things wouldn't get too weird so they'd get laid, or hoping to find their soulmate. There were probably other reasons, but she couldn't think of any others because of the way Mig was looking at her.

"We're not teenagers anymore," she finally said.

Mig reached under the table and squeezed her knee. "I'm kind of feeling like one tonight."

Chapter 19

Leah exited the Prestwich Tunnel, exhaled loudly, and rubbed the back of her neck. She'd made it through without a body dropping on the Blazer or strange shadows on the pedestrian path. Even surrounded by cars, the tension had set in the moment she passed into the gloom of the tunnel, her neck a steel rod instead of bone.

As she relaxed, Leah began making a mental list of all the things she needed to do. The adoption news had thrown her off, and she'd forgotten about calling the retired TV reporter to ask about the video of her brother's abduction. Also forgotten was the thumb drive with the underground mine tour footage. She'd intended to watch it, but the drive remained where she'd put it, deep in the side pocket of her tote bag. There was so much to do, so much to think about. And now, at the top of the list was finding a private investigator to search for her birth parents.

Gray clouds had settled in over the Dinky Minors, and the wind was blowing them her way. An early summer squall. She hoped it would hold off until she got her photos and interview.

When the enormous Prestwich Trestle came into view, she slowed. The turnout overlooking the mine was full of heavy equipment and a few cars. A man wearing an orange neon vest and white helmet waved her toward a space, then jogged alongside the Blazer as if she couldn't manage parking without his assistance. He hovered so close to the door that, if she opened it suddenly, she'd knock him down. It had to be the planning engineer. She forced a smile to her lips, gave him a little wave, then began to gather her things. By the time she'd retrieved her camera from the tote bag and stepped into the wind, he'd begun pacing back and forth.

"I was a little nervous you weren't going to make it," the man said. He was short with silver-streaked dark hair, wire-rimmed glasses, and ruddy cheeks.

Leah glanced at her phone. "I'm five minutes early. You're Rick Vale?"

He nodded, staring past her at the Dinky Minors. "It's a good thing you're early. Looks like rain is headed our way. We don't have to wait for anyone else. You're the only reporter who bothered to reply, so I'm all yours."

She wasn't surprised. The company hadn't given much notice, and it wasn't a big enough event to justify sending a reporter from Cheyenne or Denver. Even if the company sent a press release with photos and a few quotes, only the small TV stations and neighborhood weeklies desperate for news would bother running it.

The temperature had dropped, and it was chilly out. Leah would make it quick, then stop at the market in Tribulation Gulch to pick up a few things for dinner with Mig.

"Why don't we do the interview first, then I'll take some pictures. How does that sound?"

"Fine by me. I've never done this before, just so you know. So go easy on me."

The man's nervousness was contagious. She felt twitchy all over.

The work crew consisted of three men shoveling dirt at the opposite end of the turnout. Leah tapped the screen of her phone to begin recording. She'd transcribe what she needed later. Much easier than taking notes by hand. The wind was kicking up, and her hair began blowing around her face. She pulled up the hood of her jacket and held the phone several inches below his mouth. Vale looked surprised and took a giant step back.

Leah shook her head. "Oops, that's not going to work. I need you a little closer."

"Sorry," Vale said, overstepping and nearly bumping into her.

The interview lasted ten minutes. The words shot out of his mouth in a nervous jumble. Vale explained so many tourists stopped at the turnout to view the mining operation, the company wanted to make sure it was a good, safe experience. He gestured behind him. The turnout had nothing to keep people away from the edge. The yellow sign warning "DANGER, STEEP CLIFF!" went largely ignored.

The project included widening and paving the dirt lot, an informational kiosk with a roof to protect visitors from the elements, and a railing that would keep people from the edge of the cliff. When Leah had finished taking photos of the crew, she asked Vale to stand with the view of the mine to his back. She wasn't sure she'd use it, but she wanted to have it just in case.

"Would you mind standing over there for me?" she asked, raising her voice against the wind.

He nodded, then scurried off, shoulders hunched. The clouds hovered directly overhead. With any luck, she'd be done and in the Blazer before the first raindrops fell.

Vale might be inexperienced giving interviews, but he knew how to pose, down to throwing back his shoulders, tilting his head, and sucking in his stomach.

"Can you move just a bit to the right?" she asked. "I want to make sure I get the A-frame in the background."

When she was done, she came in a little closer. What she was about to do would piss off the mining company, but if she angled her camera just right, she'd be able to get a shot of the dump piles behind Vale. The piles had been there for as long as she could remember—huge mounds of gray, yellow, and red waste rock excavated from the old open-pit mine.

Vale ignored her instruction, too occupied staring at something behind her. She could hear the rumble of trucks as they climbed the steep road.

"Mr. Vale?" she called.

When he didn't answer, mouth agape now, she turned to see what he was looking at. There was nothing unusual, just a little traffic, including a big rig and two box trucks, probably headed toward the mine.

"A little to the right, Mr. Vale," she tried again.

That got his attention. He saluted and hopped to the right. She raised the camera to her eye and looked at him through the viewfinder.

Damn. He'd moved out of position, and once again, his face was contorted, like he was seeing a ghost. What the hell was he doing?

When she spun around, she realized he was staring not at the road, but at the Prestwich Trestle. Rail cars once carried copper ore over the trestle to the smelter several miles away. The structure—with its tripod-shaped platforms—was a monument of timber and iron teetering on ruin. The deck was missing enough slats to make walking across it an activity reserved for daring teenagers and tourists who didn't know any better.

Her eyes scanned the deck, on the lookout for someone about to jump—the occasional suicide did happen—but there was nothing. She'd never liked the trestle. It was creepy.

Leah turned back to Vale, who now had a hand clamped over his mouth. She glanced at the work crew, still busy shoveling dirt. The wind blew the first drops of rain into her face.

"You okay, Mr. Vale?" she said, louder this time.

He shook his head, stepping back, getting close to the edge. The man looked terrified. She dropped her camera, feeling the lanyard tug on her neck.

"Look where you're going, Mr. Vale!" she shouted.

It started raining harder. His glazed eyes were still fixed on the trestle. She rushed toward him, arms outstretched to pull him from the edge. He was only inches away now and oblivious to his precarious position. Before she could reach him, he took two more steps, and then he was falling backward. Time seemed to slow. She watched in horror as his arms windmilled, his mouth wide open in a silent scream, eyes bulging.

He disappeared over the side of the cliff.

As she advanced toward the edge, feet pounded behind her, and then a hand was pulling her away.

"Be careful, miss," a man cried.

Leah barely noticed the workmen in their neon vests. One was already on his phone. She peered over the side, a hand gripping her arm, and an involuntary cry escaped her lips.

Rick Vale had fallen on a tree growing sideways out of the cliff, impaled on a half-dead limb. Blood pooled around the wound, the rain washing it away in streaks of red. He was still alive, moaning, his limbs moving. His eyes fluttered open.

"Mr. Vale," she shouted. "Help is coming. Try not to move."

The man holding her arm tightened his grip. "That's far enough, miss. We don't want you falling too." He was a giant of a man with a gravelly voice. His face was hidden in the folds of a voluminous hood.

Dizzy, saliva thick and sour in her mouth, Leah allowed herself to be walked back from the cliff's edge. "We can't leave him," she gasped. "Can someone climb down there? So he's not alone? He could die. He can't die alone."

"One of the guys is already on his way," the man said.

Her face was wet from the rain and now from tears. "We need to keep talking to him," she cried.

But the man wouldn't budge, wouldn't release his vise-like grip on her arm. "There's nothing you can do. Let my buddies handle this. Come on now. Let's get you out of this weather." He began to pull her away.

Even though she was trembling all over, she managed to yank free. "I'm not leaving him alone."

The big man bit his lip, frowning. "All right. I have an idea, but don't move until I come back."

She nodded and watched him jog toward his truck. He rummaged around in a metal storage box and trotted back, spreading a blue tarp over the muddy ground close to the edge where Rick Vale had fallen.

"You can look over the side, but I'm hanging on to your waistband," he said gruffly. "No need to worry about me. I'm not getting fresh." He held up a beefy left hand. A thick gold band shimmered on his ring finger.

Leah stretched herself out on the tarp, already beaded with rain drops, and looked over the edge. Fingers grasped the belt loops of her jeans.

Rick Vale's glasses had fallen off, and without them, his eyes appeared swollen. The tree was three-quarters of the way down the cliff. It was far too steep for anyone to make it down without falling. Face twisted into a grimace, Vale moved his arms like a swimmer trying to stay afloat in a turbulent sea. And then Leah understood why. The tree trunk served as a resting place for most of his body, but it didn't extend far enough to support his head, and he was struggling to keep it from falling back.

All that squirming couldn't have been good for whatever was happening inside his traumatized body.

Time and weather had rounded the end of the branch that extended from his chest like some strange appendage.

"Help will be there soon, Mr. Vale," Leah called.

It seemed an eternity before two men appeared at the bottom of the hill. They scrambled up the muddy slope, grunting and cursing, their hands grasping roots to keep from losing traction.

When they'd nearly reached Vale, she shouted, "You need to support his head!"

Finding secure footing on the slope took some maneuvering, but after an agonizingly long minute, the younger of the two men found a way, shoving his work boot under a root protruding from the hill. Leah cried out in relief as she watched his hands come up and raise Vale's head. The result was almost immediate. Vale's expression relaxed. The other man stood beside him, taking his hand. She couldn't hear what he was saying, but he was talking to Vale in a soothing tone.

All the color had leeched from Vale's face. It was white. He'd stopped moving, and his mouth was opening and closing like a fish. She wondered how long he could survive.

Leah looked over her shoulder at the giant of a man still holding onto her belt loops. "Do you have anything you can throw down to help keep him warm?"

The man nodded. "I've got something in my truck, but you've got to move back."

After she'd crawled back from the edge and scrambled to her knees, her burly guardian loped toward his heavy-duty Ford. A few moments later, he was trotting back, carrying a pile of clothing. He dropped them over the cliff's edge one by one. The men below carefully tucked a sweatshirt around the protruding branch, covering Vale's neck and shoulders, another one on his lower mid-section. A jacket was gently placed over his twitching legs.

The workman leaning over Vale lowered his head until an ear was next to Vale's mouth. After a moment, he reached for the sweatshirt and dabbed Vale's eyes and cheeks with the sleeve.

"What's happening?" Leah called.

"He's crying," the workman replied.

A sob rose in her throat. Vale was trapped in a living nightmare. She couldn't imagine how terrified and confused he must be—one minute going about his job, the next staring up at the sky, rain falling in his face, a branch rising out of his chest.

Sirens wailed in the distance. Minutes later, a parade of emergency vehicles raced by. The rain eased up, replaced by a steady drizzle.

The minutes dragged on, and then emergency responders in orange jumpsuits were running toward the base of the hill. There were five of them. One clambered up the slope, while the others waited, then he slid back down the muddy embankment. The group huddled together. Leah watched as they grabbed equipment, including a basket stretcher. They scrabbled up the slope, loaded down with blankets, backpacks, and tangles of straps and carabiners. The stretcher was secured by ropes lashed around the base of the tree.

Four men supported Vale's body, while another used a cordless saw to cut the branch free from the trunk. Then, with great difficulty, they transferred him to the stretcher, branch still sticking out of his chest, and covered him with a metallic blanket. Three men went ahead to guide the stretcher down, while two more followed behind, gripping ropes attached to the stretcher. They went slowly and carefully but eventually made it down without incident.

After the ambulance left with Vale, Leah lingered in the turnout with the three workmen. They huddled together under the overcast sky in a state of disbelief.

The older of the two men, who had wiped away Vale's tears, shivered. "Rick was saying weird stuff down there. I think he was hallucinating."

Leah rubbed the side of her face. It felt numb. In fact, her whole body felt numb. "What was he saying?"

The man had piercing blue eyes. "He said he saw The Copper Man on the trestle."

The big man who'd held onto her snorted. "Oh, come on, Frank. Rick was just telling us he thinks those Copper Man rumors are just a bunch of bullshit."

Frank shoved his hands in his pockets and scowled. "I'm not making it up." He turned to the young man who'd supported Vale's head. "You heard him, didn't you, Kyle?"

Kyle stared at the Prestwich Trestle uneasily. "I heard him all right, and I wish I hadn't. All this talk about The Copper Man coming back was already getting to me, and now this."

Leah gazed at the trestle. An emotion she couldn't identify surged through her, and for a moment, she thought she saw a shadowy figure behind a diagonal beam below the deck. She was reminded of George Cunliffe coming for her brother. But then the image faded. It was just a group of pine trees in the distance.

Chapter 20

Leah looked at Mig. "He died, didn't he?"

Mig set his cell phone among the plates and Legos scattered on the table. They were in Mig's dining room, with a view of the side yard. The aspen leaves fluttered in the fading light.

"He did," Mig said, falling into the chair next to hers. "But his wife and kids got there in time to say their goodbyes. He has—had—two teenagers."

Leah pressed a finger between her eyes. The image of Rick Vale impaled by the tree branch haunted her all afternoon and into the evening. "They saw him? Like that?"

Mig scraped a hand through his curly hair, exposing a cluster of silver threads. "Apparently. The doctors couldn't remove the branch without killing him, so they pumped him full of drugs to keep him alive long enough for his family to get there."

"What a thing for them to see," she whispered.

Mig reached for her hand and massaged her knuckles. "At least he had his family around him. Are you going to be okay?"

"Eventually. Aren't you nervous to be around me? First the photographer, then Morgan. And now, Rick Vale."

Mig sighed. "It's not you that has me worried. It's all the talk about The Copper Man. It's getting out of control. We've got men who are refusing to work underground and want to be reassigned, even though they're not qualified to do anything else. Some of these guys are saying there's a ghost or something haunting the tunnels, and then this morning, we had another accident. A serious one. A contractor—with thirty years of experience, mind you—fell through an open grate between two levels. A worker who'd just finished his shift swears it wasn't open when he left. Swore it was closed. I can go on and on, but we've got a real problem on our hands, and this one isn't covered in a handbook for managers."

"Do you have any idea who's behind it?"

Mig picked up two Legos and fitted them together. "Not a clue. And all of that is off the record, by the way." He stared at her for a moment, then sighed again. "Can we make that our default setting? Off the record? Because I'd like to talk to you without wondering if I'm going to end up in one of your articles and get my ass fired."

Leah managed a weak smile. "Of course."

They fell silent, each lost in their own thoughts. The evening had gone well. Even better than she hoped. Harper, for once, had shown no shyness when they'd arrived at Mig's house. Sofia and Mason had come running to the door and pulled her toward the family room, where they'd played into the evening.

"I should go home," Leah said at last.

Mig leaned his elbow on the table, cupping his chin in a hand, gazing at her with dark eyes. "Please don't." When she didn't answer, he said, "You've already promised you'll go to the river with us tomorrow. Stay. Have a sleepover."

Leah raised her eyebrows. "With Harper?"

He gave a little shrug. "Of course."

"We don't do sleepovers," she said stiffly, sweeping the Legos into their bucket to avoid looking at Mig.

"Why not?"

"Because I don't trust other parents with my only child, and having other people's kids over is too much responsibility."

Mig cleared his throat. "That's a bit...controlling? Doesn't Harper need to learn to become independent?"

"You sound like my ex," Leah said, picking up a stray plastic panda from the floor.

"Any chance this is related to what happened to Liam?

Leah dropped the panda into the bucket. "Now you sound like my therapist."

Mig chuckled and tipped back in his chair, hands behind his neck. "Okay. What if you dropped Harper off with your mother? Then would you stay?"

Leah got to her feet and pressed her hands into her lower back. Mig watched her with a self-satisfied smirk.

"I forgot what a pain in the ass you could be." She went to the French doors and stared at the aspen leaves fluttering in the dusk.

Chapter 21

Mig's plan to take everyone for an afternoon on the river was wrecked with a single phone call. A work emergency required his attention at the mine. At her invitation, Mig dropped off Sofia and Mason at Patricia's house, where Harper waited on the porch, and they immediately disappeared into the living room. Except for delivering snacks and lunch, Leah had seen little of them.

Her mother had gone off with Shelley to the opening of the new spa. Leah peeked in on the kids. All three were kneeling in front of the boxes covered in green felt, tiny figures strewn across the floor.

"You kids need anything?" she said from the doorway.

They were so engrossed in their play, only Mason bothered to glance up.

"No thank you, Mrs. Shaw," he said.

Leah set up her laptop in the kitchen, close enough to keep an eye on the kids. Mason and Sofia seemed remarkably easygoing, but with three children, the dynamics could easily shift, and Harper could be bossy.

With the kids occupied, she searched for news coverage of Rick Vale's accident but couldn't find a single story, which wasn't surprising. Tribulation Gulch wasn't big enough to support a local newspaper, and the next largest town had already gone to print with its weekly edition and didn't have a website. Since Vale's death qualified as a freak accident, it was simply a tragic story, nothing more to it than that.

After she wrapped up one project, she started on another, then decided she'd done enough work for a Saturday. Instead, she began searching for a private investigator specializing in adoption. She found a small company with strong reviews based in Northern California, claiming to have access to public records all over the country. While the website was clear it could not guarantee a positive outcome, if they accepted the case, their website said she had a ninety percent chance of the company finding her birth parents.

She filled out the form and hit *Submit Reunion Request.*

Her phone chimed. It was Mig, apologizing that it would be another few hours before he was free, so they'd need to reschedule the river trip. After reassuring him the kids were no bother, she agreed to going to the river Sunday, followed by dinner downtown. Anything involving three young children was more of a playdate than a date, she told herself.

Her mother sauntered in at three o'clock, Shelley in tow. Leah had the impression her mother invited her friend to avoid uncomfortable adoption questions. Shelley filled the tense gaps with a breathless accounting of their experience at the new spa.

"You should write about it," Shelley gushed, holding out her hands—nails painted pale pink. "The pedicure tubs are lined with copper. It's supposed to help with aches and pains, and my feet feel incredible."

Leah stood up and stretched. "I'm not sure if there's science to support that," she said. She was a little surprised that Shelley, as savvy as she was, had bought the marketing ploy.

Shelley pursed her lips. "My parents had terrible arthritis, and they both wore copper bracelets. They *swore* by them."

Patricia poked around in the refrigerator and slammed it shut. "I didn't do the grocery shopping, and there's not much the kids would want to eat. Leah, why don't you take a turn and go to the market? Sofia and Mason might as well have dinner here. Poor Mig, having to work on a Saturday. He should join us too, if he's free in time." Her mother paused, casting a sly glance in her direction. "He's awfully handsome, and he makes a lot of mun-eeee," she added in a singsong voice.

Leah's jaw hardened to concrete. "Mother."

"You better snatch him up before someone else does," Patricia said in a silky voice.

Leah found her sneakers and put them on. "I'm going for a run, if that's okay," she announced. "Then I'll hit the store on my way back. I'll cook dinner."

Patricia sniffed. "You already went for a run."

"Not far enough," Leah snapped, snatching her keys from the counter. She pecked Shelley on the cheek and stomped toward the mudroom.

"She must still be upset about seeing that poor man fall," she heard Shelley say before the door slammed shut.

Shelley had *that* right. Leah's nightmares had become increasingly grotesque as dawn approached.

Leah drove through the small downtown and parked in the lot behind the high school. Grabbing a jacket from the backseat and tying it around her waist, she headed up a pebble-strewn trail into the hills, the same path she ran almost daily in high school. She jogged up the path, leaping over mud puddles as pine trees closed in around her, and wished she'd thought to bring a water bottle. The storm clouds had vanished, replaced by wispy fluffs of white and a full sun that warmed her face and shoulders. It was nowhere near as hot as it would get next month in July—just about the perfect temperature for running.

The scenery got better the higher she went. Leah passed a few small lakes, the air sharp with the scent of pine. At one point, she had to scramble over a fallen tree, avoiding the sharp protruding branches. Now that she'd seen what they could do to a person, it was too easy to imagine an accident leaving her helpless.

When she'd finally made it to the top of the ridge, she stopped for a moment to catch her breath and admire the view. The trees were thicker up here. Scanning the trail stretching in both directions, she spotted a dark mound several yards to her left. She crept closer.

Scat. Black bear, by the look of it. Dry and blackened by the sun. Her heart sank. She hadn't thought to bring bear spray. It had been so long since she'd wandered the hills of her hometown, she'd forgotten about the bears. Cougars, wolves, and grizzlies weren't unknown, but bear sightings were rare. There was no one else around. Coming this far ill-equipped and alone wasn't the best idea.

When she reached a small clearing, the ground began to vibrate under her feet. Leah froze, listening. No twittering of birds or skittering of small critters. The place suddenly had a foreboding air. Why had it gone so quiet?

Skin prickling, Leah looked around. Something was coming. The vibration resolved into a distinct pounding. It was coming from her right, from behind a solid wall of brush and grass obscuring whatever was headed her way.

The sound of her pounding heart whooshed in her ears. A moment later, she sensed something beyond the brush.

A presence.

A presence Leah knew wasn't human.

Branches cracked. She watched, not daring to breathe, as the grass parted.

A herd of goats crashed through the foliage and thundered toward her.

Goats! Not a bear, not The Copper Man, but goats. The herd let loose with a chorus of bleats, then continued running, disappearing into a grove of trees.

She tried to calm her sizzling nerves. This place, with its history and its stories, was starting to get to her. She couldn't even take a walk through these beautiful hills without thinking something sinister was happening.

Leah took a couple of deep breaths, then turned and coaxed her shaking legs to take her back down the hill toward home.

Chapter 22

Jogging back, Leah twisted her ankle on the uneven path. It was painful, but she could still walk on it if she was careful. She took a slightly different route, a shortcut to an old gravel road leading into town. When she emerged from a pine thicket, she saw a roughly built cabin and an old man sitting on a bench, back against a wall, petting a small goat. He had a heavily lined face covered in patchy whiskers.

"You didn't happen to see my goats?" he called.

It was The Goat Man, the one who sold his feta to the Greek Coffee Shop.

"I did see them," she said, "back near the trail. They were moving fast. I thought they would have come straight back here."

He shook his head. "You'd think, but my goats are a funny bunch. When they get spooked by a coyote, they like to hide out in a cave nearby. I lost a couple of my herd already this year. If I were younger, or in better shape, I'd set some traps."

The man grabbed a cane and pushed himself into a standing position with a grunt. He remained bent at the waist.

"My name is Theodore Spanos, but you can call me Theo. Everybody does. You look awfully familiar. You're the sister of little Liam Shaw, aren't you?"

Tilting her head to the side, Leah regarded him with raised eyebrows. "How'd you know?"

"I know everybody in Tribulation Gulch, even if they don't know me," he said with a bitter edge. "I knew who your father was when I worked at the mine, but he was too big of a muckety-muck to bother with the likes of me."

He waved his cane at the dilapidated goat pen. It looked like the animals had trampled the fence in several places. The lean-to shelter was barely standing but appeared to have fresh hay.

"One of these days, I'll get a couple of those useless teenagers in town to help me fix up this mess, but for now, I just bring my herd in at night." Theo hesitated. "You want to come inside for a glass of water?"

Leah shook her head. God only knew what it smelled like inside his cabin, if he kept his goats in there. And she was eager to get going. She needed to shop for dinner, go home, and see about her ankle. "Thank you, but if you can just point me toward the gravel road, I'd appreciate it."

The old man's shoulders slumped in obvious disappointment.

"It's right there, at the end of my driveway."

With his stooped posture and sun damaged skin, it was hard to tell, but Leah guessed he might be pushing eighty. She'd heard he'd been friends with her brother's killer. Her pulse quickened. Maybe she had time for a couple of questions.

"What kind of work did you do at the mine, Theo?" A laborer, she guessed, due to the sad state of his ruined back.

He gave a little shrug, but Leah could tell he was pleased she'd asked.

"A powder monkey, mostly." When he noted her puzzled expression, he said, "Wait here, why don't you." Without waiting for her to reply, he disappeared into the cabin and returned a few moments later carrying a wooden chair, which he set down in front of her. He went inside again and returned carrying a bundle. "Why don't you sit and put that on whatever is ailing you?"

It was a bag of frozen peas wrapped in a clean dish towel. It smelled faintly of bleach and detergent. She wondered how he did his laundry. Probably the old-fashioned way, in a steel bucket. Peeling back her sock with a wince, she saw her right ankle had begun to swell.

Leah placed the ice pack on the sore spot and looked over her shoulder at the pine thicket. "Should we be nervous about those coyotes?"

Theo gave a loud sniff. "They won't bother us. It's the goats I'm worried about. Those dummies should have come home by now. I got a rifle inside, so if you're nervous, I can go get it."

It was all too easy to imagine the old man shooting his own feet.

"I'm fine, really. You used a term I'd never heard before—powder monkey. What kind of job was that?"

The cabin sat in a small clearing. Afternoon clouds were moving in, but they were white, not the gray clouds of the squall from the day before. The sun warmed the top of her head.

It took Theo a bit of maneuvering to sit down again, a wheeze exploding from his mouth when he'd finally managed it. "It was hard and dangerous, is what it was," he began. "We drilled holes, some of them thirty feet deep, then shoved in a few sticks of dynamite. If everything worked right, we'd be hiding when they went off, and rocks would come shooting out of the hole, like bullets from a rifle. And then we'd do it again, as many times as we needed to blast out a large enough chamber. That's the old-fashioned way of doing it. I was the last of the powder monkeys."

Adjusting the ice pack, Leah cleared her throat. "You knew The Copper Man, didn't you?" she said, then held her breath.

Theo thumped his cane on the ground. "If you mean George Cunliffe, then yes, I did." The words came out harsh and fast.

Leah nodded but didn't rush in to fill the silence.

Theo's face seemed to sag. "I guess I still have a hard time believing the George I knew was capable of such terrible things. He killed your brother, and I don't want you to think I'm making excuses for him. I saw that TV show they made about George, but they didn't talk to me, or I'd have set them straight. George was shy, but he was no loner. He had friends, just not the muckety-mucks. Mostly ordinary fellows like me. He grew up on a ranch, and he liked being outdoors more than anything, collecting rocks and such. I used to help him out at his ranch, when he needed a hand. But something inside him must have snapped. He couldn't take it no more. The George I knew was a broken man but a good one." Theo ran a hand over his face and sighed audibly.

Leah leaned forward. "Was it the death of his son?"

"Yes, but it was more than that. A lot more."

"Like what?"

Theo held a single finger in the air. "The company did him dirty, for one. They messed around with the water supply somehow, and one day, all the wells on his property were poisoned." A second finger went up. "For another, that meant

166

his property was worthless." Theo snapped his fingers. "Just like that, it happened. George had already spent most of his savings on the land, fixing up the old house and buying the cattle, and he'd already quit his job at the mine. The company threw some money at him, but not enough to make up for the damage they did. Then, they had a hard time finding someone as smart as George to replace him, so I heard, and they offered him a bunch of money to get him to come back. They had him by the balls, excuse my language, so you can imagine he wasn't too happy about it."

Theo picked at a hole in the knee of his worn jeans. "George was also mad about other things. The way the mine was polluting the air and the company refusing to do anything about it. And he was worried about the state of the tailings ponds, but whenever he tried to bring it up, they wouldn't give him the time of day. When his son died, that pushed him over the edge. George told me plenty of times his son died because of the poison in the air, and with his asthma, it killed him, plain and simple."

Leah felt a vein on her temple twitch. "So, in retaliation, he killed five children."

Theo hung his head. "There's no denying that. Revenge is what he was after, pure and simple, but that don't justify what he did." After a moment, he lifted his chin and sniffed. "You've heard about all the bother down at the new mine? All that talk about a ghost?"

"Something like that," she said cautiously.

Theo's eyes narrowed. "You're not a believer, then?"

"In ghosts? No."

"Ghosts, spirits, what have you," Theo said, waving his cane around. "After what I saw when George died, I tend to believe those sorts of stories, as far-fetched as they may seem to you."

Something in the man's tone made Leah's chest go tight. "What did you see?"

A faraway look came to the old man's eyes. "I was the one who found George Cunliffe's body. In fact, I saw him jump. I was doing some cleanup in one of the yards that day." His shoulders came up around his ears, and he shuddered. "God almighty, it was a sight. I've never seen anything like it, and I hope I never do again. He fell into some tailings water, and it turned him an awful color. If you've never been near tailings, let me tell you, it stinks. When he opened his mouth to try and say something, I had to stop myself from turning away, it was that bad." He ran a hand over his eyes. "George wasn't quite dead when I got to him, and when he passed, I was right there holding him. That's when I had the most awful feeling. It was like all the anger bottled up inside him passed right through me. It took me a while to settle down after that. I've seen dead men before, Miss Shaw, and all I can say is, something wasn't quite right about him, or that expression on his face. It wasn't natural."

"So, you're saying you believe the men at the mine?" Leah said. "You think there's a ghost."

"No," Theo said slowly. "Not *a* ghost. The ghost of George Cunliffe. I think sometimes he comes around to check on me. And that's what scares my goats."

Chapter 23

Leah was in the kitchen, making sandwiches, when her mother walked in. Patricia had spent Sunday morning as she usually did—attending church, followed by breakfast with Shelley and their friends.

"What's all this?" her mother said, gesturing at the assembly line of sandwich fixings on the counter.

"For our picnic to the river. With Mig and the kids. I told you we were going to go yesterday, but Mig had to work."

Her mother was wearing a navy-blue dress topped with a white sweater, legs encased in pantyhose. She was the only woman Leah knew who still wore them.

Patricia tossed her keys onto the table. "I thought you meant next week. You can't go today. What about your ankle? And we're going to the opening of the amusement park."

Leah dropped the knife on the cutting board. Her mother had reminded her earlier in the week, but with everything going on, she'd forgotten all about it. She had to go. Her mother had served on the committee for the new tourist attractions, and after all the babysitting Patricia had done, the least Leah could do was show up to support her mother.

She looked down at her ankle. "The swelling is down. I don't think I sprained it. And I'm sorry, I just forgot. Brain fart. I wouldn't miss it for anything. But listen, do you have a problem if I invite Mig and his kids? I feel bad letting them down on such short notice."

Her mother bit her lip, then exhaled loudly. "It's fine. I can get extra tickets, and it'll be nice for Harper to have friends her own age there."

Leah reached Mig before he'd hitched the boat to the truck. His response pleased her.

"No problem. We can go next weekend." He lowered his voice. "Maybe even get you to do that sleepover. And I've heard about the amusement park. Apparently, there's a train ride. People at work have been talking about it. It sounds like fun. How about if we get pizza in town on the way back?"

"Perfect," she said. Patricia had plans for the evening, so Leah didn't have to worry about her.

Leah wrapped up the sandwiches and stashed them in the fridge.

When Mig walked through the door wearing a red and white checked shirt and cowboy boots, she laughed.

"You got a lasso to go with that?"

With the three kids carting Harper's booster seat to Mig's truck, they were alone in the house. He pulled her close.

"I wouldn't call it a lasso," he said, breath hot in her ear.

Leah felt a delicious flood of warmth.

A noise at the door made them leap apart. It was Harper.

"Oh," she said, then turned on her heel and left. From the living room, she shouted, "I was just looking for Chicken, but I found her!"

"We should probably tell them something," Mig said, scraping his hand through his hair. "So they're not confused."

Leah's eyebrows shot up. "Tell them what?"

Mig pointed an index finger directly at her, then used it to bump his chest. "You and me. Like, going out. Boyfriend and girlfriend—whatever people our age call it. I don't even know."

She barked out a laugh. "You're getting way ahead of yourself."

Mig frowned. "I'm old enough to know what I like. And I like you. Why waste time when we can get this going. Whatever this is."

He made it sound perfectly reasonable, except for one thing.

"I'm not ready to rush into anything," Leah said.

"That's fine." Mig knocked his hip into hers. "I'll do all the rushing. You can take it easy."

He peered out the window facing the street.

"Wow, they're already in their car seats, ready to go." He turned to face her. "Can you stop overthinking this, Leah? Unless you're really trying to tell me you're not interested, now or ever." Mig placed his hands on her shoulders.

Wearing boots, she was his height.

Her insides went all melty. "I didn't say that."

Chapter 24

The Tribulation Copper Railroad was a mile outside of town. Patricia had talked about it, but Leah was not prepared for its size and scope. It was a full-blown amusement park, with a fake Western town, including a ticket kiosk and an artfully landscaped path leading to rail cars made to resemble old-fashioned mine trolleys.

The park was already crowded with families. The weather had cooperated, delivering a clear but chilly Sunday afternoon hovering at fifty-five degrees.

Mig stood in line with the children to buy hot chocolate at the Old West Chocolate Shop, while Leah took in the sights, ankle still sore from her hike.

While she waited, she took some pictures. The Old West town had a jail, a shooting shack—not yet open but taking reservations—a prospector's shack, a saloon with whiskey tastings, and a two-story museum devoted to the history of the Prestwich Copper Mine.

Leah spotted her mother in a small crowd gathered in front of the museum but couldn't catch her eye. When Mig returned, handing her a steaming cup of mocha, he was accompanied by a smiling young woman. The kids sat on the wooden sidewalk, legs dangling over the edge, sipping their drinks as they looked around.

"This is Gabby Sartu," Mig said. "We work together. She's one of our mining waste engineers."

Gabby had tawny skin, dirty blond hair pulled back in a long braid, and freckles across her nose. No makeup, Leah noticed. A natural beauty.

"Oh, then you must be working on the plan for the tailings pond," Leah said.

"Yes, we're getting to that soon," Gabby said, looking surprised.

Mig waved his hands in front of Gabby. "Don't say another word, Gabby. Leah's a reporter." Slinging an arm around Leah's shoulder, he added, "And you, it's a day off for all of us, so don't even think about interrogating her."

As much as Leah hated being told what to do, she found herself leaning into Mig and laughing. "Okay, okay. Guilty. I promise not to grill your co-worker."

Gabby smiled, revealing a gap in her teeth, which added to her charm. Leah liked her immediately.

"Gabby's going to be the first to go on the zip line," Mig said.

She wriggled her shoulders. "It's my thing. I couldn't believe they were opening one here. I've done Hawaii, Las Vegas, the Ozarks, the Grand Canyon. Okay, those were *way* bigger, but still. This is very cool."

"She's crazy," Mig said with a shudder. "I hate heights."

"There's a zip line here?" Leah asked, looking around and still not seeing anything.

Gabby pointed to a tower in the distance. Leah recognized the shape—an iron headframe from an abandoned mine, painted a dull red. It resembled an oil derrick. As far as she knew, the old Prestwich Copper Mine hadn't needed one because it operated on the surface, but there were plenty of the relics around the state, and it made a fitting zip line tower. A platform had been constructed at the top.

"Where does it go?" Leah asked.

"Across the rail tracks, over a creek, and through the woods past the old settlement," Gabby said, pulling up the collar of her fleece jacket.

Leah squinted at the platform. "Are there seats on that thing?"

"No. It's the kind with a harness." Gabby glanced down at the phone in her hand. "Oops, I better get going. They want me to hear the whole safety talk, even though I told them I've been doing this since I was thirteen. Nice to meet you, Leah." She ran off.

"She's nice," Leah said.

Mig sipped his coffee. "She's a character, and a damn good engineer. We were lucky to get her."

Leah glanced over at Harper. The kids were digging into a paper bag. She watched as Harper pulled out a churro.

So much had happened over the last week, it felt like a hundred loose threads dangled just out of view, things left undone and unexplored. A serious talk with her mother about her adoption. Checking the video the TV photographer shot during the mine tour, right before he died. And verifying whether or not there was video of Liam's abduction.

She told Mig what old Theo had said about The Copper Man returning as a ghost. Mig scowled.

"That's what the miners seem to think too. We're consulting a workplace psychologist to see if they can help us figure out what's going on. It's bordering on some sort of mass hysteria."

If that was the case, it qualified as a legitimate news story, which would be tricky to do, given her relationship with Mig and the information he'd revealed off the record. Leah pushed away the thought. It was Sunday. She deserved some time off.

When the kids had finished their snacks, they explored the park. The kids loved the jail, and Leah took some pictures of them in a cell, gripping the bars, looking appropriately solemn.

Patricia waved them down as they walked past the museum. "There you are. The gunfight is about to start." She took Harper's hand and pulled her onto the wooden sidewalk, then motioned for Mason and Sofia to join them.

Leah stared at her mother. "Gunfight?" she echoed.

Before her mother could respond, music began blaring. It was a tune that evoked dry dusty trails and cowboys on the range. Then, saloon doors banged open, and two men in vests, neck bandannas, and cowboy hats came storming out, where they were met on the street by two women wearing outfits worthy of Calamity Jane. The two sides faced off and began exchanging fake fire, smoke filling the air.

Harper tugged at her hand. When Leah glanced down, Harper said, "Gimme says it's not real, Mom. Don't be scared."

Sofia watched the gun battle with hardly a blink, taking tiny bites from her churro. Mason, on the other hand, had his head buried in his father's thigh, arms wrapped around his legs. The little boy's body jerked with every shot fired.

Mig swung Mason onto his hip, his son's dark curly hair blending with his own. "It's just a show, buddy," Mig said. "Those guns aren't even real."

Mason responded by punching his father's shoulder. "I'm not scared. I hate loud noises. They hurt my ears."

"I hate loud noises too, Mason," Leah said, rubbing his back.

To her surprise, he reached out and took her hand, gripping it tightly. She gave it a squeeze. They stood, connected like that, for the duration of the gunfight, which went on too long in Leah's opinion, but the crowd seemed to love it. When it finally ended, two men and two women lay in the street, then leaped to their feet to a round of applause.

"That was wholesome fun," Leah said.

Mig laughed. "Maybe they'll hang a cattle rustler for an encore."

Harper came around to stand in front of Leah, her heart-shaped face scrunched in disapproval. "Why is Mason being a baby?"

Leah stared down at her daughter in surprise. It was the first time Harper had resorted to her usual, censorious self since meeting Sofia and Mason. "Harper, that's not nice. Some people have sensitive ears, like me and Mason. That gunfire was so loud, they should have handed out earmuffs."

"Mason is afraid of the dark too," Sofia said.

Harper shook churro dust off her hands. "I'm not."

As Sofia turned to Harper, frowning, Mig cleared his throat. "Everyone is scared of the dark. At least a little."

Before Harper could launch into an explanation that would surely unsettle her new friends, Leah flagged down her mother. Patricia made a ceremony of distributing train tickets to the kids, then announced, as guest of honor for the opening ceremonies, she was riding in the front car and invited the children to sit with her. Mason took a little cajoling to leave Mig, but when he saw the yellow and green train pull into the station, whistle blowing, steam billowing from the engine, he went happily enough.

Mig took Leah's hand as they watched her mother march the children toward the depot. "I guess it's just you and me, then."

"I guess it is," she said.

As they waited to board, Mig said hello to at least a dozen people, all employees at the mine. Most had brought their families.

They sat in the second to last rail car, open to the sky. The conductor, a young woman also doing double duty as tour guide, launched into a peppy talk about the history of the narrow-gauge train and the one-and-a-half-mile loop through a pine forest, past a ghost town from the late 1800s.

With the first part of the track on a gradual incline, the train progressed slowly, steam gushing about the wheels, a series of whistles and bells accompanying its departure from the platform. As it picked up speed, the steam engine began to make its signature *choo-choo* sound.

Leah hoped Mason wasn't panicked by the noise, and she wished she could see Harper's face. It was her first train ride. She texted her mother asking her to take a few photos, and her mother responded: *Of course!*

Mig introduced her to a co-worker sitting directly across from them.

The middle-aged woman with a blond bob said, "Oh, Mig, is this your wife?"

Leah's leg spasmed, and she choked a little on her coffee.

Mig wasn't rattled. He chuckled and said, "This is my girlfriend, Leah Shaw." Then he squeezed her knee and followed up with introductions.

The woman was chatty, so when the conversation turned to the new payroll system, Leah's attention drifted back to the scenery. They were passing through a dense thicket of trees, the branches forming a low canopy overhead. A sprinkle of pine needles fell around them.

The train began to slow. Over the speaker, the conductor said, *"We're about to enter the settlement of Camp Griswold, named after Gerald Griswold who founded it…"*

The woman's grating voice was getting on her nerves. High, thin, and overly enthusiastic. Leah would have a headache by the time they were done.

When the train entered the clearing, it slowed so everyone could admire the old, rustic buildings and take pictures. There was something eerie about the small, dilapidated structures out in the middle of nowhere. No effort had been made to repair the buildings, but great care had gone into the grounds. Ore bins, wooden frames used to drag loads over the land, and wheelbarrows were staged on crude plank platforms.

But an art installation took Leah's breath away—a copper statue of a miner surrounded by a small field of pickaxes, pointed ends sticking up like strange, dangerous weeds.

A ripple of whispers reached her ears. "The Copper Man!"

Leah's stomach lurched. As she twisted in her seat to get a better look, her hand was so clammy, it slid on the railing. Her mother had served on the planning committee for the tourist attraction. How could she have allowed such a thing to happen?

The statue didn't resemble George Cunliffe, but it didn't matter. That it was a statue made of copper was enough.

The train stopped. The copper statue was just off to her right.

The tour guide was saying, "*And this beautiful statue, created in Denver, is based on the only known photograph of Gerald Griswold...And oh! I'm going to need to interrupt myself because we have something very exciting headed our way. If you look up, you'll see cables from our new zipline ride. I'm hearing that in just a moment, we'll be seeing the very first, brave rider zipping by...And there she is. An employee at the New Prestwich Mine!*"

Leah jumped to her feet to get a better look, squinting at the top of the thicket from which they'd just emerged. A cable ran over the tops of the trees, secured to a series of tall, narrow platforms. If Leah had to guess, the cable was about the height of a four-story building. Way too high for her liking.

A figure appeared in the distance, dangling from the cable by a harness. It resolved into Gabby in a bright red helmet. She whizzed toward them, yelling and whooping.

Mig laughed. "Someone's having fun."

The sun was in Leah's eyes. For a moment, Gabby appeared oddly fuzzy, as if a shadow passed over her. It gave the impression of a faint dark film enveloping the young woman.

Leah clutched Mig's arm. "Did you see that?"

Before he could reply, she heard a sharp metallic sound.

The lanyard attached to the harness came to an abrupt stop. Gabby's legs jerked up violently, then over her head, spinning the young woman into a backward somersault. The harness snapped. Gabby's body fell through the air, body bent into a U-shape, arms flung behind her, down toward the statue and straight into the field of copper pickaxes.

People began to scream.

"Jesus Christ," Mig shouted beside her.

Gabby's head was at a strange, unnatural angle, face turned toward Leah, eyes open but unseeing. The force of her fall had thrust her body down on the points of several pickaxes, piercing and tearing at her mid-section. Parts that belonged inside her lifeless body erupted through the yellow fabric of her sweatshirt. The young woman lay in a pool of blood and viscera, her long braid stained a dark red.

Chapter 25

As soon as the traumatized riders had been taken off the train, Patricia whisked the children home. Luckily, Harper, Mason, and Sofia hadn't seen Gabby fall to her death, nor the horrific sight of her broken body impaled on the copper sculpture. Neither had Patricia. All four had been sitting in the car closest to the engine, farthest from the accident. Mig had run to the front and ordered them to stay put, and for once, Patricia hadn't tried to take charge. She'd kept the kids from following the others ignoring the conductor's pleas to remain seated.

A large crowd had gathered around Gabby, eyes wide, hands pressed against mouths. One man fainted. A woman slumped to the ground, crying. Eventually, park employees managed to get everyone back on the train, and it returned to the depot.

People milled around in the plaza near the saloon and shops. A couple sat on a bench, consoling their sobbing daughter. They'd been in the rail car ahead of Leah.

An announcement came over the speakers, asking everyone who'd been on the train to stay on the premises until deputies arrived, while everyone else was asked to leave immediately.

Mig put his arm around Leah's waist and guided her to the saloon—where he bought them both a shot of whiskey. He downed his, then left her at a small table near the window and went outside to call his manager. She could see him pacing on the wooden sidewalk as he talked. When he was done, he bent over, hands on his knees. Mig stayed like that for a long time before coming back and falling into the chair across the table. His skin had a gray tinge to it.

"What do you think happened?" Leah finally asked.

Mig shook his head. "I don't know. There was so much blood, I couldn't tell what was going on with the harness, but it looked to be intact. If I had to guess, something went wrong with the lanyard attachment. I don't know what would cause it to stop so suddenly like that."

She sipped the last of her whiskey. "Did you see anything when Gabby was coming toward us? On the zip line?"

"Like what?"

"Like a shadow, or something. It's hard to explain, but it was like a dark cloud was around her for a fraction of a second."

"No. I didn't see anything like that."

Leah glanced at the table next to her. Two men and two women, who appeared to be around thirty, were whispering and holding out their phones. She could guess what that was about. In the chaos and confusion as passengers gathered around Gabby, she'd seen some people taking photos.

"I think the situation at the mine is about to get worse," Leah said, jerking her head in the direction of the foursome.

"What do you mean?"

"Gabby's accident is all over social media."

Mig rubbed the side of his face and groaned. "Shit. Of course, it is. This is why you're so good at your job. I'm going outside to give my boss a heads-up."

Leah logged on to WiFi and saw that the gory images were already trending, some with the worst parts blurred out but most unedited. She was too shaky to contact her editor, or the producer at the cable network, but it was just a matter of time before they heard about what happened and called her. They'd expect a story, and she'd have to deliver.

After deputies and paramedics arrived, it was her turn to explain what she'd seen. She left out the bit about seeing a shadow. Mig hadn't seen it, and in the breathless first-person accounts she'd seen on social media, no one else had either. It must have been a trick of the light, like when she'd stared too long at the maze of triangles that formed the Prestwich Trestle after Rick Vale fell off the cliff.

While they were driving home, her editor called, then Rhonda, the producer, asking if she'd heard about the zip line accident. When she admitted to witnessing it, both clucked their concern about her mental health, but she could imagine them punching the air, thrilled they had a reporter in the right place at the right time.

The web story was easy enough. File the copy and photos as soon as possible. She hadn't taken any of the accident, but that wasn't a problem. There were plenty on social media they could use with proper credit.

Rhonda surprised her by announcing Crystal was already enroute from Denver.

"The morning show is all over this, so you're going to have to file a story for them too," Rhonda said. "They wanted you to go live, but I said it was too soon for that." She paused. "But Leah, you're going to have to do a stand-up. If you can't, you need to let me know now. No backing out at the last minute. It's my reputation too."

Ouch. She'd deserved that.

When she'd chickened out of doing a stand-up for the last story, she'd let Rhonda down—the woman who'd championed her regular guest appearances on the cable news network. And all because she was afraid some faceless assholes might take issue with her size and troll her on social media. If she let her fear take over, she'd never get the reporter job Rhonda was pushing for, and the money and benefits that came with it.

"Of course, I'll do it," Leah said, with more certainty than she felt.

"Good," Rhonda replied briskly. A long silence followed. "Leah, you can do this. Whatever is going on in your head, tell it to fuck off."

Before she had a chance to reply, Rhonda hung up.

"You have to cover this?" Mig asked.

Leah looked out the window. They'd just crossed a bridge with a creek running under it and entered a stretch of dry rolling hills. "I do."

Mig squeezed her shoulder. "Are you up to it?"

"Not really, but it's my job. Usually, I don't have to cover these kinds of stories, so it's not been an issue. Until now. But no matter what kind of reporter you are, if you happen to be on the scene of breaking news, it's just something you've got to do."

When they arrived home, they found Patricia drinking tea and reading a book in the kitchen. Somehow, she'd talked the children into watching a video, and all three had fallen asleep in a nest of blankets. Mig said he'd wake the kids and take them home, but her mother wouldn't allow it.

"Let them sleep. They're fine here. Shelley and I were planning on taking Harper into town this afternoon, get her mind off that horrible thing. Why don't you let us take Sofia and Mason?"

Mig went home to join a video call with company headquarters about the accident. Leah was about to go up to her room to begin writing, when she remembered what had troubled her on the train ride.

"Mom, did you know about that copper statue?"

Patricia stared at her over the top of her book, a new one about Ronald Reagan. On the cover, the actor-turned-president was smiling and wearing a cowboy hat.

"I certainly did not. I wasn't on that committee. That was all somebody else's doing. Somebody new in town, with more money than sense. And no one else had the brains to put a stop to it." Patricia wrinkled her nose. "So, now they're all upset that people are calling their brilliant idea 'The Copper Man.' You've never seen so much hand-wringing."

"You must have been shocked," Leah said.

"You can say that again."

In her bedroom, Leah called the sheriff's office and asked if they had any updated information on the death of Gabby Sartu. She was transferred to a press officer. Gabby's family had been notified, so her name and age had been released to the public. The incident would be investigated by the federal Office of Safety and Health Administration. The zip line attraction would remain closed until further notice.

Writing the article as a first-person account was easy enough. The script for TV turned out to be a bigger challenge because she only had what she'd shot with her phone that day, which included the main zip line tower but not Gabby in her harness and helmet, or any of the awful video of her accident. What Leah needed to make the story work were eyewitness accounts other than her own—it was, after all, national television.

She scrolled through her phone, looking for posts about the accident, then checked the profiles. Leah was surprised to see that Zoe, the server from the Greek Coffee Shop, had been there. Somehow, she'd missed her in the crowd. She also recognized Marcy, the bartender at Boxcar Willy's Saloon. Both would make excellent on-camera interviews, if she could get them to agree.

Leah messaged them and within ten minutes had received replies. Both were willing to speak, despite some jitters about being on TV. She warned them it might be late by the time the photographer got into town, but in the meantime, she asked for five minutes of their time on the phone. Doing a pre-interview would give her a sense of what they had to say and allow her to write the script in advance, shortening the turnaround time.

Neither woman had seen anything Leah hadn't, but both did an excellent job expressing their shock and disbelief watching the young woman plummet to her death and the unusual way she'd fallen.

By the time Crystal texted to say she was in downtown Tribulation Gulch, Leah was freshly showered and made-up, with a script ready to go. There was plenty of light in the early evening sky. She grabbed the jacket she'd worn earlier in the day and put it on, then drove to meet Crystal at the Greek Coffee Shop.

While she waited in front of the restaurant, her hands and feet tingled with cold. Leah shoved her hands in the fleece-lined pockets. Something small and hard met the fingers of her right hand.

She plucked it out.

It was a copper nugget.

Her spine lit up, tingling. She hadn't put it there, she was certain, and she didn't think Harper, her mother, Mig, or the twins had either.

A nugget appearing so soon after another horrific death felt like some kind of sinister message.

Unmoored, legs weak, Leah grabbed hold of a lamp post to keep from drifting into unreality.

Chapter 26

The interviews with Zoe and Marcy went well. Both women were still emotional from the horrific accident they'd witnessed and described the scene and the crowd's reaction with just the right amount of detail.

Monday morning at eleven, after a night of horrible dreams about zip lines and copper nuggets, Leah met Crystal at the turnout overlooking the mine to shoot her story. She sat beside Crystal in the satellite truck, watching her edit, but it wasn't the story Leah thought she'd be writing.

Overnight, a video made by a college student in Laramie had gone viral. He'd watched the documentary about George Cunliffe, happened to see Leah's photo alongside articles she'd written, and put the pieces together. He confirmed she was the sister of Liam Shaw, The Copper Man's fifth and final victim, and the author of several recent stories about deadly mishaps linked to the mine.

Sue, her editor, had blown up her phone before Leah had had her first cup of coffee. Next thing she knew, she was "invited" to a video call with Sue and Rhonda. The news outlets often partnered on stories, including this one.

They watched the first several minutes of the video together, then Rhonda paused it and asked Leah if the allegations were true.

The excuses Leah gave sounded lame, even to her. She might have mentioned "trauma" and "PTSD" a few times but, in the end, apologized for not confessing earlier.

"So *that's* why you didn't want to do the mine story," Sue said.

"Pretty much," Leah admitted.

Rhonda continued playing the video.

The college student announced he'd been contacted by a group of miners planning to stage a walkout to draw attention to strange things happening underground, things the company didn't seem to be taking seriously. Leah's insides shriveled as she watched.

Leaning into the camera, the young man with green eyes and green beanie said, "*So, what we've got here is a brand new modern mine that cost, like, billions of dollars, where every day of production is really important because, you know, money, and some dudes in hardhats are saying, 'nope, we don't want to work because there's a fucking ghost and we don't feel safe.' And if that isn't crazy enough, we've got four weird deaths. Four! Let's take a look. First up, a photographer fell and died during an underground tour the day before the mine opened. Guess who was on that tour? Leah Shaw, sister of Liam Shaw, the final victim of The Copper Man serial killer. Weird death number two! The new PR woman for the mine fell onto a car leaving a tunnel and died. Very mysterious. Guess who was driving that car? Leah Shaw! You're going to love this next one. An engineer at the mine fell off a cliff and was impaled on a tree, as in skewered by a branch! Guess who was there that day, interviewing him, when he fell? Wait for it…Leah Shaw! And that's not the last time you're going to hear me say her name. Because the woman who fell off the zip line for no apparent reason? The one who just happened to fall onto a bunch of pickaxes? Well, guess who was there and saw it all go down. Leah Shaw!*"

Her photo flashed on the screen each time he said her name.

The video blogger paused to take a deep breath. The theme song to the *Twilight Zone* began to play, and he wriggled his fingers in front of the camera. *"Don't ask me what all that means, but it's weird. Really weird. It may all be a coincidence, or there could be something really, really strange going on with…Leah Shaw."* His voice was altered for that last mention of her name, made to sound demonic with a deep voice and heavy echo.

"Well, shit," Rhonda said.

Sue had pressed her hands against the sides of her head as if to keep it from exploding. "Leah, I'm so sorry about your brother. I simply do not have the words. That is beyond anything I can imagine. As for what we just watched, we do not have to dignify it with a response. He's not a member of the credible media, and to be perfectly honest, as ridiculous and annoying as the whole thing is, it's going to drive a lot of traffic to our site. Doesn't exactly hurt ratings either, does it, Rhonda? Leah, do you think there's anything to that walkout? Because if there is, that's the story you should be doing."

Leah ground her teeth. Scooped by a college kid in Laramie. A low in her career. "I'll make some calls."

Which was how Leah found herself in the satellite truck with Crystal, rushing a story for the cable news channel. She'd managed to track down the miner organizing the protest, and they'd interviewed him and a couple of others that morning. The company refused her request for an on-camera interview, instead issuing a statement condemning the walkout and dismissing the allegations of supernatural activity as "ludicrous and devoid of factual merit." But, the statement went on, the company had retained the services of a workplace psychologist to meet with the concerned employees.

"This is such a crazy story," Crystal said, fingers flying over the keys. Later, after she'd had a chance to watch the college student's video herself, she said, "No wonder you don't like talking about your childhood."

As they shot her stand-up on the turnout, far from the edge where Rick Vale fell, Leah straightened her shoulders, focused on her enunciation, and stared directly into the camera.

After two takes, Crystal gave her a thumbs-up. "Nailed it."

Leah's moment of pleasure was fleeting. Her attention shifted to the Prestwich Trestle. The thing was so huge and ominous, her eyes kept sliding past Crystal to the mesmerizing pattern of triangles, seeing shadows where there were none.

Mig texted: *Stuck in meetings. Saw the video. Hope you're OK. I'll buy wine. See U tonite.*

Inside the satellite truck, Leah was pleased with how she looked on camera. Without someone standing next to her, or anything to show scale, she didn't look like the giant she'd imagined. Tall and imposing maybe, but not anything approaching freakish.

More importantly, Rhonda was thrilled with the results. She texted: *OMG! You're a natural. The exec producer is going to love you.*

Crystal yawned and said she was headed back to the hotel for a nap. "Rhonda wants me to hang out for another day or two, just in case…"

Leah finished the sentence in her head. Just in case there was another fatality. Just in case the cable channel's future reporter found herself at the center of a story that could attract millions of eyeballs.

Crystal drove off, leaving Leah sitting in the Blazer, scrolling through social media. Her stomach clenched when she saw her name trending as a hash tag. Since she'd last checked, she'd received what looked like hundreds of messages. Leah tossed her phone onto the passenger seat and headed toward the west end of the Prestwich Tunnel.

It was three o'clock. Too early for a shift change at the mine, too late for the usual influx of people traveling to the river to fish.

Cars streamed out of the tunnel. Lots of SUVs, some with kayaks and storage boxes strapped to the roof. While she waited at the red light, she peered at the hill above the tunnel. She couldn't see the trail from where she sat, but it was up there. The arched entrance was sandwiched between columns of concrete, giving way to retaining walls on either side that kept rocks and dirt from falling into the road. A concrete lintel topped the opening. She'd never paid much attention to it before. It formed a protruding ledge over the mouth of the tunnel—wide enough for someone to stand on. If Morgan had jumped, that had been her launching point.

She shuddered at the thought.

Leah glanced in the rearview mirror. No other cars had pulled up behind her. It looked like she might be the only car heading east. She couldn't remember ever going through the tunnel solo, and she didn't relish the drive ahead, alone in her truck, alone in the dim confines of the tunnel.

Her skin went clammy. The light turned green, and she stepped on the gas.

Without a car ahead to lead the way, she flicked on the high beams and proceeded slowly. The tunnel seemed to stretch on forever. If the walls weren't so close on either side, she'd gun it and race through.

Leah hadn't gone more than five hundred yards, when the yellow lights flickered overhead. Her windows were still down. Over the constant roar of the giant fans, the faint rush of water could be heard from the trench below the pedestrian walkway.

The lights went out.

From the ceiling came a loud clanking, the fans stopped, and all was silent and completely dark.

"Damn it," Leah cried. Her headlights illuminated the next four hundred feet of roadway, but the pedestrian walkway remained inky black. So black that if a person were walking there, she wouldn't see them.

Leah was alone in the tunnel. No other headlights had appeared in the rearview mirror. As much as she wanted to get out of there, she forced herself to maintain a slow and steady speed. It was dark, nothing more. Just like driving on rural roads at night.

With the power out, it was quiet in the tunnel, except for the noise of the tires on the road. She rolled up her window. Whatever had caused the lights to go out, she hoped it was temporary. Wrestling with thoughts of shadows on the walkway, just feet from her car, Leah gripped the wheel tighter, eyes squinting for a glimpse of daylight ahead. It felt like she was crawling.

A dull thud came from the roof of the Blazer.

Leah jumped, foot slipping from the gas. The Blazer slowed. She listened, ears straining. It was hard to hear anything over the wild beating of her own heart.

Another noise on the roof brought goose bumps to her skin. It sounded like something was walking up there. Whatever it was, she didn't want to see it. She had to keep driving. The high beams cut through the blackness.

Something slid down the windshield.

Leah slammed on the brakes, heart racing, a cry escaping her throat.

A figure was standing in front of the truck.

It was no road worker coming to her aid, no vagrant in search of a nap in a darkened recess of the tunnel.

The figure was completely still, a ruined face watching her. Leah took in its reddened, oozing skin, the slightly leftward tilt of the nose, what passed for eyes that fixed on her own.

Her hands lifted off the steering wheel and came up in the air, like a plea.

The dreadful shape did not move. A horrible liquid drained from the ghastly terrain of its face. She felt the intensity of its anger coming at her in waves.

It wasn't human. Now. But it once had been.

Leah didn't know how long she sat there. The windows fogged up. But even though she couldn't see it, she knew it was still out there. The thudding of her heart was the only sound as her mind reeled, trying to figure out what to do. An entire minute passed.

Then, the fog on the glass cleared.

One by one, the overhead lights flicked back on. The road in front of her was empty.

The figure had gone.

Something glimmered on the hood of the Blazer, inches from the windshield, close enough for her to see it clearly.

A copper nugget.

In that moment, she knew.
The Copper Man was back.

Chapter 27

Leah didn't remember the drive home, but somehow, she made it. As she stumbled toward the house, Shelley came running out to meet her in the driveway.

"I've been waiting for you" she said, clutching Leah's arm. "Something terrible has happened."

The shock of seeing The Copper Man had muddled Leah's brain. Why was Shelley at her mother's house?

And then she remembered. Shelley and her mother had taken Mig's children and Harper for an outing somewhere.

Leah pressed a hand against her chest, suddenly tight and strangely heavy. "What happened?"

"We can't find Harper and Mason," Shelley sobbed. "I've been trying to call you."

Leah glanced down at her phone. No missed calls. There was no service in the Prestwich Tunnel. Another layer of dread descended, squeezing her throat.

"Were you near the river?" Leah asked, imagining Harper and Mason at the water's edge, sending a toy boat filled with plastic dinosaurs on a ride. Harper had taken swimming lessons, but she would be no match for the cold, rushing water.

Shelley shook her head. "No. We were at the park near the Dinky Minors. They went to the bathroom and never came back."

Near the mine, then. Out near George Cunliffe's old house—where he'd lost his only son to an asthma attack. An icy chill swept through her. Neurons fired like a hundred tiny lightning strikes.

"My mother let the kids go to the bathroom alone? What the hell was she thinking?"

"We were the only ones there!" Shelley cried. "And it wasn't very far from where we were sitting."

Leah took a deep breath. Lobbing accusations was a waste of time. "Have you called the sheriff's office?" she asked, climbing back into the Blazer.

"Of course. They're probably there by now. The kids can't have gone far."

Leah had to go. The journey would take her back through the Prestwich Tunnel, but there was no way around it.

"Does Mig know?"

"He's already on his way."

A pounding on the driver's door made them both jump.

Leah peered through the window and saw Colt Carter, the owner of Hook 'Em, dressed in hiking pants and a jacket covered with pockets.

"I'm headed up to the park. The sheriff's office put out a call for volunteers who know the area, so a bunch of us are on the way. If the kids are where we think they are, we'll find them."

Leah pressed a finger in the space between her eyes. "Where do you think they are?"

Colt adjusted the baseball cap on his bald head. "If they wandered a bit too far, it's possible they might have fallen into an abandoned mineshaft. There's plenty of them out there. As in dozens. I'm part of a group that goes around sealing them.

Our coordinator, who's been at it the longest, is probably there by now."

"Jesus." Leah gripped the steering wheel.

Colorado had a similar problem. She'd written about it. Mine shafts hidden in the nooks and crannies of the Rocky Mountains could run hundreds of feet deep. Sometimes, they were filled with pools of water, but they could also hide toxic air, old explosives, bats, snakes, mountain lions, and other predators.

Colt studied her through narrowed eyes. "You're in no condition to drive, and neither is your friend, here. Why don't you come with me?"

The thought of driving the Prestwich Tunnel after her Copper Man experience made that an attractive offer. Leah climbed into Colt's Yukon.

As they approached the Prestwich Tunnel, she stuck her head between her knees.

"You okay back there?" Colt called from the front seat.

"Panic attack," she said, words coming out in a wheeze.

Not exactly a lie. More of an omission. If she were to tell her companions about The Copper Man, they wouldn't believe her. No one in their right mind would. Her thoughts slid to the past, to the Fourth of July Rodeo Carnival 1985, to a hooded George Cunliffe carrying off her brother. Now that she'd seen him, or what was left of him, she was convinced he'd taken Harper and Mason.

The picnic area was in the foothills below the Dinky Minors. When Colt pulled into the lot, Leah spotted Mig standing next to a sheriff's deputy, carrying Sofia. Her head was buried in his neck. The sky was a brilliant blue, with just a few wispy clouds floating over the ridge. Two red-tailed hawks circled overhead.

She ran to Mig. "Anything?"

His mouth had a strange set to it, stretched somehow. "No."

Leah absently patted Sofia's back while scanning the area for Patricia. "Does Sofia know anything? About where they went?"

Sofia lifted her head. Her face was puffy and red from crying. "They went to the bathroom and didn't come back," she wailed.

Leah took in the playground made of wooden structures resembling an old mining town. She immediately understood why her mother had chosen to bring the kids to the out-of-the-way location—it was a little gem of a playground, surrounded by benches. There was even a gazebo. A small stone building at the far end of the park had to be the bathroom. There was no fence to separate it from the rolling hills stretching beyond it.

From Mig, she learned a few more details. Her mother, Shelley, and the kids had been the only ones at the park. When Mason had to go to the bathroom, Harper offered to go with him. Patricia had seen Harper go into the girl's bathroom. When five minutes had passed and they hadn't returned, Sofia had run over to fetch them and came back carrying one of Mason's green Crocs. Panicked, Shelley and Patricia checked the bathrooms, then searched the surrounding area, calling the children's names. Another green Croc was found several dozen yards up a slope. That's when they'd called for help.

A team of two dozen people were scouring the hills, and so far, there had been no sign of the children.

Leah scraped a shaking hand through her hair. "Where's my mother?"

"Out looking," Mig said. "I should be too but…" His voice faded as he moved Sofia onto his other hip.

Sofia clutched his arms, sniffling.

"Do you think she'd be okay with Shelley for a while?" Leah whispered.

Mig tucked a strand of Sofia's hair behind her ear. "What do you think, Sofia? Would you mind staying with Shelley for a bit while Leah and I look for your brother and Harper?"

When Sofia nodded, Mig strode over to Shelley, Leah on his heels. Shelley was helping a woman unload bottles of water and grocery bags filled with snacks.

"Of course, she can stay with me," Shelley said. "Sofia, can you help us organize all this food for the people looking for your brother?"

Even at her young age, Sofia looked relieved to have something to do and began laying out energy bars and bags of trail mix on a folding table.

Leah and Mig set out toward the hills. She wished she'd taken the time to change into hiking boots, but she'd be okay, unless the terrain got too steep.

"Has Harper ever wandered off before?" Mig asked.

She was breathing through gritted teeth as they climbed the hill, trying to calm her jangled nerves. "Not like this. Has Mason?"

Mig didn't hesitate. "No. Never. He's too timid. Sofia is the brave one. I don't get this. Shelley said they didn't see anyone else. I guess someone could have been waiting in the bathroom, but taking both kids? At the same time? *I* can barely carry them both at once. And where would someone take them?"

Wherever George Cunliffe took the children before he'd killed them, Leah thought. The location had never been discovered, or if it had, the investigating officers had never revealed it.

That's what scared her most. The thing that materialized in the tunnel had been George Cunliffe, not a ghost. The Copper Man had a physical form. Unless she'd imagined the whole thing, that made him some sort of monster. Something beyond her understanding.

Leah felt a powerful need to tell Mig what she'd experienced, but she couldn't. Not now.

Instead of answering Mig's question, Leah asked one of her own. "Did you talk to the volunteer who knows about the abandoned mines? What did they say?"

Mig's face appeared tense and slightly gray in the sun. "I did talk to her, just for a minute. She knows where most of them are. She even brought a map and handed out copies to the rescue team." He stopped to help her over a fallen tree. "But again, why would the kids come up this hill on their own? That doesn't sound like them, does it?"

"No," she said grimly.

Leah wanted to scream, grow wings, and fly over the hills with eyes as sharp as a bird of prey. She dragged her nails over her face, just to feel something other than terror. If Harper had somehow fallen into a mine shaft, would she wait for help? Or, unafraid of the dark, would she explore its dark recesses in search of a way out?

Maybe, all those years ago, George Cunliffe had found one of those shafts, and that's where he'd slit the throats of his victims.

The incessant whine of ATVs came from somewhere over the ridge, a team of first responders on all-terrain vehicles.

Leah stepped on a loose rock and went sprawling. The heels of her palms skidded on the pebble-strewn dirt. When Mig hauled her to her feet, her hands were bloody and raw, but she barely noticed. He dabbed at them with the end of his shirt.

"Oh God, where are they?" A sob caught in her throat.

He took her arm, and they continued. After several minutes, she heard a shout.

Mig jerked to a stop, throwing an arm in front of her chest in an automatic reflex to keep her from running toward the sound.

"We found them!" a woman's voice shouted.

More people began calling out, and in the distance, Leah heard boots thudding on hard ground.

They raced toward the commotion, Leah reading everything into the tone of the excited voices. Relief, mostly. They were alive. They had to be alive. She gave a little cry as a group of people came into view, standing in an area below a rocky outcropping covered in sage brush.

Leah's pulse raced as she spotted the entrance to a small cave.

"Are they all right?" she cried as she ran toward the cave, ignoring the stitch in her side.

A moment later, a woman wearing a white helmet and orange half-zip top appeared, carrying Harper, body limp, eyes dazed. Out of the gloom of the cave, a man followed, Mason wriggling in his arms.

Under the streaks of dirt, Harper's heart-shaped face looked nearly bloodless in the afternoon light. As Leah stood over her, tears welling in her eyes, Harper blinked in recognition.

"Is she hurt?" Leah asked, breathless.

"I don't think so, physically," the woman said. "Nothing seems to be broken."

Leah held out her arms. "Can I take her?"

The woman smiled. "Of course," she said, gently placing Harper into her arms.

Leah cradled her daughter like a baby, legs dangling—an awkward position, but Harper allowed it, burrowing her head into Leah's chest, breath hitching.

"Hey, sweetie," Leah said. "You're okay now. You're safe. I've got you." The words were as much for her own benefit as they were for Harper's.

If the rescue team hadn't found them, her daughter and Mason might have languished in the cave, too hungry and dehydrated to find their way out, and her child would have been lost to her forever.

Leah bent to kiss the top of Harper's tousled head. "You're such a brave, brave girl, sweetie."

Harper pressed harder into Leah's chest and began to sob. "It was scary in there. I don't like the dark, Mom."

Chapter 28

Neither Harper nor Mason could remember much from their time in the cave.

"When I finished using the bathroom and was waiting for Harper, a man was there. Out of nowhere. He scared me because he looked like a monster. There was something wrong with his face, and it was a bad color, and he smelled. I closed my eyes and held my nose," Mason said.

Harper nodded. "When I came out of the bathroom, I saw the man carrying Mason over his shoulder up the hill. I didn't see him before, but he looked like a bad red monster. I ran after them to the cave. I became really tired and fell asleep. When I woke up, my head hurt, and I didn't know where I was, but Mason was there too."

"Did he touch you?" the medic had asked.

"Only when he carried me," Mason said. "He showed us a big knife and did this." He mimicked slicing his own neck.

Both children had small spider bites but, other than that, had no injuries.

Patricia had pressed her fist against her mouth and kept repeating, "I don't understand," as Shelley led her to a quiet spot to recover.

Leah understood well enough. She knew the sinister monster who menaced her in the tunnel had taken the children. Maybe that's why he was there, to gloat. Several times, she came close to confessing her tunnel experience to Mig, but she couldn't bring herself to say the words. She'd seen George Cunliffe's ghost, or whatever the hell he was, but how could she expect Mig to believe such an outrageous story?

Their children had suffered an emotional trauma, and her little confession might even be seen as some sort of Munchhausen by Proxy—a way of trying to attract attention back to herself. So, she said nothing.

While a listless Harper sat in the bathtub, Chicken staring dolefully from the lid of the toilet, Leah searched the pockets of Harper's dirty clothes for a copper nugget. When she didn't find one, she let out a tremulous exhale of relief. She didn't know why they randomly appeared in the house, or in her pockets, or on the hood of the Blazer, but she guessed they were meant as a calling card. Or a threat. Pretending to cut his throat in front of the children had been threat enough. And yet, he hadn't harmed either of the kids.

The events of the day had proved too much for Patricia, who blamed herself for the abduction, and she'd shut herself up in her bedroom, where she'd knocked herself out with sedatives.

Mig texted to say Mason was having a rough time and had spent an hour on a video call with his mother, begging her to come home from Mexico.

Leah called her ex-husband. Jason couldn't believe his ex-mother-in-law had allowed Harper out of her sight long enough to be abducted. Leah couldn't either, but after seeing Patricia's near-catatonic reaction, she decided it was unnecessary, and even heartless, to castigate her mother.

They had an early dinner of soup, crackers, and ice cream, then Harper's eyes began to flutter closed. By seven o'clock,

Harper drifted off to sleep in Leah's lap in the big easy chair in the living room, snuggled under a throw. They sat together like that for an hour, Leah thinking, listening to her daughter breathing.

The ghost of George Cunliffe, or whatever he was, could have killed the kids if he'd wanted to.

When he was a living, breathing man, he'd murdered five children, including her brother, as revenge for the death of his son. Somehow, Leah had escaped him the first time, and he'd slit Liam's throat instead, but now he was back. He'd terrorized her daughter and Mason with a knife but hadn't carried through on the threat.

Maybe The Copper Man meant it as a message to *her*.

Leah thought back to that terrible day, the day her mind refused to recall in entirety. Childhood trauma was the doctor's explanation for the gaps in her memory, but there was still something *off* about what she could and could not remember. She thought back to her neglected to-do list. Her brother's abduction might have been captured on video by a TV reporter who then denied its existence.

Did the video exist or not? She had to know, once and for all.

She'd call the reporter, Bill Kimball, tomorrow. In the meantime, there was another video she could watch immediately.

Leah carried Harper, gently snoring, upstairs into her own bedroom. She tucked her daughter in, then rummaged around in her tote bag. Leah found the thumb drive with the footage of the underground mine tour, plugged it into her computer, and put on her headphones. She angled the chair so she could keep one eye on Harper while she watched the video.

First, she skipped through everything shot above ground. Watching as the cage descended into the mine was enough to make her itchy all over. She had to swallow repeatedly to quell the sick feeling as Daniel the photographer fell and cracked his skull against a steel vat. Several times, she appeared on camera, glancing nervously about, and once, looking startled.

Going only on instinct, she decided to rewatch only those sections. If the mayhem happening in Tribulation Gulch was somehow related to her, maybe Daniel captured something odd around her.

Nothing. Nothing.

And then, something.

So fleeting it was, no wonder she hadn't caught it the first time.

As the camera swung past her in the tunnel, it stopped, capturing her startled expression. She remembered that moment, wondering if Daniel intended on asking her a question on camera, but he hadn't. Seconds later, he'd trained the camera—shakily—on Randall, the TV reporter, instead. But the camera panned toward her again. Daniel zoomed in to the tunnel wall behind her. Through the headphones, she could hear his sharp intake of breath, followed by the blood rushing in her ears.

Caught in Daniel's camera light was a figure lurking in a dark recess. It resembled the shape that had loomed in front of the Blazer in the Prestwich Tunnel, except it was fuzzy and surrounded by a reddish glow. Its face was blurry, like a smudged watercolor, and gave the impression of dark holes for eyes and melting, stretched skin. And then it was gone.

The image lasted half a second. Long enough to have startled Daniel. It explained why he kept pointing the camera in her direction. Obviously, he'd hoped to capture whatever it was he thought he'd seen.

Leah hit play, holding her breath as she watched the segment again, this time frame by frame. The camera angle revealed what she'd missed the first time.

The Copper Man was staring directly at *her*—not Daniel. It was as if he'd been *willing* her to turn around and see him.

Goosebumps broke out on her arms.

Fuck.

She stood, snatched her phone from the nightstand, and went into the hall. Leaving the door open several inches, she called the retired reporter, Bill Kimball.

He picked up on the third ring.

"Mr. Kimball, my name is Leah Shaw. I'm—"

"I know who you are," he interrupted in a hoarse, wheezing voice.

Leah paused, surprised. "Then do you know why I'm calling you?"

"I'd guess it's about the rumor that I shot video of what happened at the Rodeo Carnival all those years ago." He paused and took several heavy breaths. "I can tell you that's just a rumor. There is no video."

Leah considered her next words carefully.

"Mr. Kimball, I respectfully ask that you hear me out. What happened back then was the most horrific thing a family can endure. I've lived thirty-five years not being able to remember what happened to my brother, and if there is any way to learn the complete story, I am determined to find it. But you need to know something else, something even more important. Someone kidnapped my daughter today. She's six, just a year older than my brother, Liam, when he died. Her abductor threatened to cut her throat, and I need to know why. Why her."

A swift intake of raspy breath, and then the sound of something falling over. A glass, maybe. "What happened to her?"

"We found her," Leah said, leaning her head against the bedroom door frame. The mound in the bed that was Harper shifted, revealing a spray of dark hair spread across the white pillow.

"Oh, thank God," Kimball whispered.

There was a long silence. Leah let it stretch on.

Finally, he said, "I don't understand. George Cunliffe is dead. Are you saying there's a copycat killer now?"

"Maybe. Maybe George Cunliffe really didn't die that day. I don't know. There are a lot of things I don't know. But I am sure of one thing. He—or someone— went after my daughter for a reason, and they'll do it again, so I need all the information I can get to help solve this fucking mystery. If you have a video in your possession, Mr. Kimball, now is the time to tell me, and if anything happens to my child and you've not done the right thing, then whatever happens is on your head."

Kimball was silent for so long she feared the call had dropped. She checked her screen.

Still there.

"Can you help me, Mr. Kimball?"

At last, she heard a cough.

"All right," he said wearily. "I'll send you what I have. Please call me after you watch it. But know, I never wanted you to see it, Leah. I hope you understand when you watch it. And I'm warning you. You're going to see something you're not expecting."

He took a long, rough breath, then exhaled into the phone. "And you're not going to like it."

Chapter 29

The video Kimball uploaded to a file sharing site awaited.

Leah ate two power bars she found in her tote bag and chased them down with water from a plastic bottle. When she'd run the tap in the bathroom, the water gushed a reddish-brown, the acrid odor making her eyes water. Another message from The Copper Man. Leah was hungry and could use a proper meal, but she didn't want to leave Harper alone upstairs.

She moved the desk and chair so both faced Harper. If her daughter happened to wake, Leah didn't want her catching a glimpse of whatever she was about to watch. She clicked on the link Kimball sent to her email and hit play.

Bill Kimbell, as a young reporter, knew how to frame a camera. He'd positioned himself on a hill overlooking the event grounds to get some establishing shots.

The mutton busting contest was scheduled during the rodeo's intermission. Leah had been the third rider and, hands desperately gripping the animal's long wool, had managed to stay on the back of the sheep for eleven seconds. Her brother, Liam, was scheduled for the second half of the event, but he refused to ride, coming up with all sorts of excuses. His stomach hurt. His helmet didn't fit right. The safety vest was too big and scratched him under the chin. All except the real reason—he was terrified.

215

Leah remembered her parents arguing about it. Her mother had said if Liam didn't want to ride the sheep, then he shouldn't be made to, but her father had been adamant. If Leah was brave enough to do it, then her *brother* should be too.

Leah remembered her mother's fury and the final look Patricia shot her way just before storming off, alone. As if somehow, the whole situation had been Leah's fault for doing so well.

Kimball had caught her ride on video, explaining that afterward, he'd walked up the hill to get a wide shot with the intention of shooting the rest of the contest, since mutton busting was a crowd favorite. He was panning across the barn, when two small children emerged, running. A little boy followed by a girl.

It was Liam, wearing a shirt in red paisley, and Leah, auburn hair secured in two pigtails, a pink top, and fringed bull riding chaps over jeans. Liam stopped abruptly and whirled around to face her, whipping off his helmet and flinging it aside. Their height difference was startling. She'd forgotten how much taller she'd been.

Liam was shouting soundlessly. Grownup Leah watched as her younger self leaned slightly forward, hands on hips, and stomped a booted foot. The memory of their argument came flooding back.

Liam told Leah he thought mutton busting was stupid, then had run away from their father while he'd been distracted chatting with friends. At first, Leah was insulted, then alarmed that Liam had gone off on his own. Their parents had warned them about The Copper Man, and she knew if they wandered away like bad children, he might get them. When Leah couldn't get her father's attention, she decided to fetch Liam herself.

Little Leah grabbed Liam by the arm and tried to drag him back toward the barn, but Liam managed to wriggle free. He was walking backward, one hand out in front of him in a warning to stay away.

They were in a secluded area, a large dirt patch between the back of the barn and a row of sheds. A figure appeared around the corner of a building and froze when he saw the children. It was a man, dressed like so many of the others at the rodeo carnival, in jeans and a tan shirt.

Leah was saying something, and Liam spun around. The man was unwrapping something from around his waist. A long, shapeless jacket. Slowly, as if they were small woodland creatures he didn't want to frighten, the man put it on and pulled up the hood.

The sight of the hooded figure seemed to galvanize Leah into action. She darted forward, grabbed Liam by the arm, and with a mighty jerk, nearly hauled him off his feet. Stopping, she gave him a little shove toward the barn. Clearly, she was trying to get him to run.

The camera jerked upward. There was a brief view of the sky and then the group again.

"*Hey!*" Bill Kimball had shouted off camera. "*Hey you!*"

With all the noise coming from the barn, and the distance, it was obvious the man and the children couldn't hear him. It was also obvious, from the way the camera bounced, that Kimball didn't know what to do. Drop the camera and find a way down the bluff to intervene or keep filming?

The hooded man remained where he'd first appeared, looking around, clearly nervous someone would come. When no one did, he strode toward Leah, one hand stretched out in front, beckoning.

Then Leah was shouting at Liam.

"It's The Copper Man!" she remembered screaming. Because she knew it was him.

The camera was on the move now. Bill Kimball grunted as he ran down the slope. More sky. Shots of sheds. More warning shouts from Kimball that George Cunliffe didn't seem to hear.

The video stabilized enough that Leah could see what happened next.

Liam's body twitched, as if coming alive to the danger, and he turned, boots scrabbling in the dirt. They ran together for a short distance, and as she usually did, little Leah pulled ahead with her longer stride and stronger legs. When she'd reached the back of the barn, and safety, she realized Liam was no longer at her side. Turning, she saw—as if in slow motion—the hooded figure reach out, grab Liam, and throw him over his shoulder.

For a moment, little girl and man stared at each other, and then he was bounding away.

All of that happened in seconds. The video ended abruptly, with the camera dropping and the sound of feet pounding on the dirt.

"I think he meant to take me," Leah said, phone in hand. She was sitting cross-legged on the floor, just outside her bedroom.

Bill sighed. "I think so too."

She ran a hand over her face. "I left Liam. I ran, and I just left him."

Another sigh, this one louder. "No. You were just a little kid, and you were scared. You were running for your life. You did nothing wrong. At first, I thought he must have been your dad. Or a relative. It took me a while to figure out what was really going on. If I ditched the camera sooner, I might have got down that hill faster."

"You were too far away," Leah said. She squeezed her eyes shut. Pressed the phone against her ear so hard it hurt. "I pretty much left Liam for dead. I as good as killed him." She hesitated. "Did you show the video to the detectives?"

"I did, but George Cunliffe killed himself the next day, and there was plenty of evidence he was guilty. The lead detective made the difficult but understandable decision not to enter it into evidence."

Leah shook her head. "I don't understand. Why? Why would he do something like that?"

The house was eerily silent.

"Because of what happened when he took you home," Kimball said. "Your mother was hysterical. She was out of her mind with grief. The detective said your parents' behavior concerned him, almost to the point of contacting someone at social services." He paused. "When they brought you home, your parents didn't pay you any attention. They seemed incapable of doing much, in fact. They didn't try to comfort you. They couldn't see past their own pain. My friend was concerned if your parents saw the video, they might hold it against you, and he didn't want to be responsible for something like that."

"I see," Leah whispered, hardly able to breathe.

She did see. Leah saw all the way back to the past and how it connected to the future, at least as far as her mother was concerned. She understood the remoteness, the distance between her and her parents after that day. Her mother's refusal to talk about her adoption.

Her parents had probably wished The Copper Man had kidnapped their adopted daughter, rather than their flesh-and-blood son.

"Are you all right?" Kimball asked. "Do you have anyone you can talk to about this?"

"Yes," Leah lied. "I'm fine."

Chapter 30

After climbing into bed next to Harper, Leah stared up at the ceiling, thinking.

The Copper Man wanted something. He'd been following her since she got to Tribulation Gulch, starting with his shadowy appearance in the Prestwich Tunnel on their drive into town. People she'd met—all associated with the mine—died in a series of bizarre accidents. Then, he'd taken Harper and Mason but allowed them to live.

What did The Copper Man want?

When she needed answers for a story, she picked up the phone or scheduled an interview. Well, she needed answers now, but there was nobody to call.

What the hell did he want?

Revenge. That's what he was after in 1985, when he killed five children. Now that he'd returned, why would things be any different? But if he was after revenge, why wasn't she dead already?

It took her a long time to fall asleep, and when she finally did, she dreamed she was at the bottom of a mine shaft, George Cunliffe looming above her, holding a hunting knife covered in her blood.

A knocking noise came from the top of the shaft, and suddenly, she was wide awake, listening.

Leah bolted from the bed, heart thudding. It was 3:00 a.m. Outside, the wind whistled. But the noise had nothing to do with the weather outside. It was coming from somewhere down the hall.

She opened the bedroom door, reached around, flicked on the light, and peered out.

The hall was empty. The bathroom door was closed, and so was the door to Liam's room at the far end.

Leah tiptoed toward Liam's room, skin crawling. The knocking sound was louder. She could hear it distinctly over the howling wind.

Tap, tap, tap.

Through the lone window in the hall, a white pine swayed in the gale, illuminated by the porch light. As Leah approached the door to Liam's room, her feet encountered a patch of wetness. She let out a yelp and jumped back.

In the dim light, a reddish-orange liquid oozed from under the door.

The door was unlocked.

Leah took a breath and pushed it open.

Liquid covered the floor from one end to the other. It poured from the top of the freshly painted walls where they met the ceiling, coming down in rivulets. An acrid odor stung her nose. The lid to Liam's toy chest was open, and above it, copper nuggets swirled in the air. Every few seconds, one would break out of formation and strike the wall.

Tap. Tap. Tap.

The nuggets rose in a steady stream from the box.

All the hairs went up on her skin.

There was something else in the room.

What she saw made her grasp the doorframe with trembling fingers—a shadow lurking in the open closet. She stared at it, blinking, and watched as it resolved into the hideous shape of The Copper Man.

A copper nugget whizzed toward her, striking her on the neck. She gave a little cry as she registered the stinging pain. A second nugget hit her square on the hollow at the base of her throat. When the next ones came, she raised her arms, and the nuggets pelted the sleeves of her sweatshirt.

Leah spun around to run from the room, from The Copper Man, when the assault stopped as suddenly as it started. The shadowy figure had moved, now standing between her and the hallway. She opened her mouth to speak, but no words came out.

The horrible figure from the Prestwich Tunnel hovered there. Not a ghost. Something between a badly disfigured man and a monster. There was a limit to what the human mind could comprehend, and the ghastly thing standing before her was beyond that limit.

Leah lurched back, lost her footing on the slick floor, and fell on her backside. She stared up at Cunliffe's ruined, oozing face, half hidden under the folds of his hood. Leah froze, just like the first time she'd seen him at the rodeo carnival, but this time, the fear was clearer, sharper. This time, there was no question the hooded stranger was bad. He was worse than she could ever imagine, and no longer human.

Cunliffe slowly raised a hand.

Leah scrabbled backwards, the heels of her palms slipping on the wetness. Rolling to her knees, she was pushing herself up, when a copper nugget struck her on the cheek. The pain was sharp and searing.

When she looked up, The Copper Man was gone.

Chapter 31

Leah hated the way Mig was staring at her—warily.

"You have to believe me," she said. She felt like a character in a bad movie. They'd talked for nearly an hour, but she'd failed to convince Mig she'd seen The Copper Man. Twice.

Mig moved to the open door and watched the children playing in the backyard.

She lowered her voice to a whisper. "Mig. We have to figure out what he wants."

Mig slowly turned to face her, brown eyes dull. "Who? The man you said is a ghost, or maybe a monster, who was once a serial killer but has come back from the dead? Leah, as much as I want to believe you, it's not easy."

"It's not easy for me either," she hissed. Leah raised a hand to her cheek. The copper nugget had left a gash where it struck her, a bandage covering the wound. It still stung. "Why would I lie about something like this?"

His expression shifted to a pitying look. "I didn't say you were lying, Leah. What happened yesterday scared the holy hell out of us, but come on. How am I supposed to believe…all of that?" His eyes took in the bandage and the welts on her throat, then he looked away.

Did he think she'd intentionally hurt herself in a pathetic bid for attention? Leah gripped the edge of the kitchen table, face flushing. "Because I'm asking you to, for me. For the sake of my child, and yours. He took Mason too, so God only knows what that means. Come with me back to the house and see Liam's room for yourself. It's a fucking shitshow."

Mig shook his head. "I am not going ghost hunting." He took a few deep breaths, and when he spoke again, his voice softened. "Look, there's only one thing I'm sure of, and it's that this isn't a safe place for the kids. I'm not sure what the hell is going on, but with all the crazy stuff happening, I've made some calls. I'm getting the twins out of here. And I think you should do the same with Harper."

"Where are you taking them?"

"To their aunt in Arizona. I've called my ex. She's flying back from Mexico as soon as she can get away."

"But Mig…"

His gaze never left her face. "I think this has all been too much for you, Leah. You've been through a lot, but no matter what is going on, we have to get the children away from here."

Leah wrapped her arms around her stomach, winded by the meaning behind his words. He was speaking to her as if she was having a mental breakdown, appeasing her with gentle logic.

"You need to trust me, Mig. Please."

Mig held up a hand. "If you'll keep an eye on the kids for me, I need to pack up their stuff."

Mig was right. They had to get out. There was nothing to keep her in Tribulation Gulch. Rhonda, her producer at the cable channel, had sent Crystal and the satellite truck to cover another story in Colorado.

Leah had to put distance between The Copper Man and Harper. She drove around town, agonizing over the choice, as Harper dozed in the backseat.

If Mig didn't believe her, she could only imagine how her mother would react. Patricia's connection to George Cunliffe was deeply personal. He'd murdered her only son. Expecting her to believe Cunliffe had risen from the dead was inconceivable.

Whisking Harper away without notice wouldn't be easy. It seemed cruel to separate the two, but staying in Tribulation Gulch was no longer an option.

At home, she found her mother in the kitchen, still wearing her robe, staring off into space, a cup of tea at her elbow. Leah felt a flicker of unease at the sight of her disheveled mother.

Harper stirred beside her, tugging at her sweater. "What's wrong with Gimme?"

Patricia turned to Harper and blinked slowly. "Oh, Gimme is just feeling a little tired this morning, darling." She rubbed her face. "I must have slept too long."

Leah crossed the room and touched the back of her hand to her mother's forehead. "Mom, you're warm. Have you taken your temperature?"

"Am I?" Patricia asked faintly. She used both hands to push herself up from the table, then dropped heavily back down into the chair.

Leah hurried to the bathroom, returned with a thermometer, and pushed it into her mother's mouth. A few seconds later, it beeped.

"Mom, it's a hundred and two. You need to get in bed."

Patricia gave a weak nod. "It must be the darn flu. This thing is hitting me like a truck." She flapped a hand at Harper, who was walking toward her with a pout and outstretched arms. "No, darling, you'll have to stay away from Gimme for a while. You don't want to catch whatever I have."

Her mother's flu was a complication, but not enough to derail her plan. In fact, it might make it easier. After she'd tucked her mother into bed with ginger ale and saltines on her nightstand, Leah said, "Mom, I hate to do this, but I have to go back to Denver. Like, right away. I'm sorry, but it's work."

Her mother struggled to lift her head from the pillow. "That's good. It's probably better that you go." Puffy eyes slid toward the doorway, where her granddaughter hovered. Lowering her voice, she added, "I was going to suggest it anyway, after yesterday."

"But first, we should call a doctor. Is there an urgent care in town?"

Patricia's head fell back onto the pillow. "No. Trib Gulch is too small for that. Listen, why don't you call Shelley and see if she can come over. That way, you don't have to worry about me. You should get a move on, before it gets too late."

It was a seven-hour drive to Denver. Leah could make it tonight, if she drove straight through, but there was no way in hell she was taking Harper through the Prestwich Tunnel and chancing another encounter with The Copper Man. That meant taking a longer route home, but that was a tolerable inconvenience.

Harper followed her upstairs, shoulders slumped. "But I don't want to go," she wailed. "I want to stay with Gimme, and I want to play with the twins."

Leah shoved her laptop in her tote bag. "I know, and I'm sorry, sweetie. But Mason and Sofia are going to visit their aunt in Arizona. We'll come back to see Gimme as soon as we can, okay? And you'll get to see Daddy too. Won't that be nice?"

Harper's mouth pinched tight, but she nodded.

By the time Shelley arrived, Leah had everything packed, along with a lunch box with snacks and water for the road. She checked her phone. Nothing from Mig. Liam's wreck of a room remained locked. Leah had done what she could, mopping the upstairs hallway. When her mother was feeling better, she'd call and make something up, like pipes leaking in the walls.

Harper threw her arms around Shelley's knees and stared at Leah with accusing brown eyes.

"Okay, sweetie, time to say goodbye," Leah said.

On the way out of town, Leah's eyes darted across the landscape. She half expected The Copper Man to appear or drop another body on the hood of the Blazer, maybe send a herd of stampeding goats to block her way. She was so preoccupied, she missed the turnoff. Leah quickly ruled out making a U-turn. The new route would take her past Riverton and Sweetwater Station, but she wanted to put as many miles between them and Tribulation Gulch as she could.

Harper was uncharacteristically quiet. When they finally passed the sign for Fort Steele, she said, "Can I have a night light in my room, like Mason?"

"Of course, you can, sweetie," Leah answered. "We can pick one out together when we get home."

As they passed through a grove of cottonwoods, Elk Mountain just ahead, Harper said, "Did the police find the bad man who left us in the cave?"

"No, not yet." The next part was the truth and a lie. "But they're working on it." The sheriff's office could investigate and search all it wanted, but it would never find the real culprit because he was beyond their reach.

When Harper began to complain her bottom hurt from sitting too long and asked about dinner, Leah decided to stop overnight in Laramie. They'd traveled three hundred miles. That should be enough to put them out of George Cunliffe's reach. She chose a generic but clean-looking hotel on the main road, new construction with bright lights and interior hallways. Leah asked for a room on the ground floor, closest to the front desk.

"We lock the doors at eight o'clock," the clerk said, a woman of about fifty, with bangs and antler earrings. She lowered her voice. "I understand your concern, traveling alone like you are. But don't worry. I've lived here all my life, and it's safe here."

They ate dinner at a cafe with exposed brick walls. When the server brought Harper's mac and cheese, her daughter took one look at it and covered her face. "Yuck. It's got junk on top of it."

Leah scraped off the breadcrumbs and handed Harper a fork. Harper stared at the dish with suspicion before spearing a single macaroni.

"It's good," she said, eyes widening.

Leah sampled a bite. It tasted and smelled delicious—with a hint of sherry and garlic. Fancy for Laramie. Her Thai chicken salad was every bit as good.

Back in the hotel, she helped Harper change into her pajamas and tucked her into bed. The room had white walls, a striped carpet in blues, rusts, and yellows, and modern, cartoonish paintings of elk, antelope, and deer.

"I'm just going to go to the bathroom and wash my face," Leah said.

"Leave the door open." With Chicken tucked beneath her chin, Harper aimed the remote at the TV.

Leah was tempted to take a hot shower but didn't want to leave her daughter alone, so she made do with running a hot damp towel over her chest, arms, and legs, then carefully washed her face, avoiding the bandage and tender spots on her neck. She was patting herself dry when Harper screamed.

Leah shot out of the bathroom so fast, she tripped over a pile of clothes on the floor. When she got to her feet, Harper was sitting bolt upright in bed, pointing at the drapes. The long and heavy curtains were moving, like there was something behind them.

She should have yanked the curtains back and revealed whatever was there. That was the obvious thing to do, but all the bones in Leah's body had turned to ice water.

It's him, she thought. *He's here.*

Harper bounced on the bed behind her. "Mom?" she whispered.

Something was opening the drapes, parting them enough so she could see the window. The glass was smeared with a thick, reddish-brown goop oozing down the glass and dripping onto the carpet.

But no one was there.

Something glimmered on the window ledge. Copper nuggets formed a pattern on the freshly painted white wood. Words.

GO HOME.

The Copper Man had left a message. George Cunliffe was not restricted to Tribulation Gulch. He didn't operate by any rules. Wherever they went, so could he. It had taken him less than five hours to find them.

"What is it, Mom?" Harper cried.

Leah gripped the back of a chair and took a deep breath before answering. "There's a vent on the floor," she said, voice hoarse. "The air was coming through it and moved the curtains."

Harper's eyes were fixed on the messy window. "What's that?"

"A bird must have hit it," Leah said. "That's a little blood, I think. Let me close the curtains so you don't have to look at it."

Harper stuck out her tongue and made a gagging noise. "Eww, that's so gross."

The cell phone rang, and Leah jumped.

Harper crawled to the bottom of the bed where Leah had left it and stared at the screen. "It's Mig," Harper announced. "I want to talk to the twins. I want to tell them about the dead bird."

"Let me say hello to Mig first," Leah said. Her hand shook as she answered the call. "Hey. What's up?"

Mig was breathing heavily. "Leah," he finally said. "Something just happened." Mig sounded dazed.

"What? Where are you?"

A long silence followed. "Evanston. We were headed to Salt Lake in the morning. I had us on a flight to Phoenix." He cleared his throat. "Where are you?"

"Laramie. What do you mean, you *were* headed to Salt Lake?"

"Leah, you were right. I saw him. The Copper Man. The kids had just fallen asleep, and when I came out of the bathroom, a man came out of the wall. I don't know how to explain it, but he stepped out of the wall, and he was a mess, and his face was fucked up, and he was holding a knife." Mig's breath hitched. "Please tell me I'm not crazy."

Leah collapsed into a chair. "No more than I am. When did it happen?"

"A few minutes ago."

"Was there anything else?" she whispered.

"Yeah. I took a picture. I'll send it."

Her phone chimed. She swiped at the screen. There was no need to enlarge it. Giant, muddy red letters on a white wall read: GO HOME.

Leah was terrified, but in a strange way, she was also relieved. Relieved enough to croak out a short, harsh laugh. At least Mig believed her now. At least she wasn't alone in believing the world had monsters in it. And why and however this was happening, they were in it together.

"He was here too," she said. "Did you find any copper nuggets?"

A long silence followed. "Two of them." Mig sighed. "On the table next to the kids."

Her stomach lurched. "Shit." Leah turned her back to Harper, who'd lost interest in the curtains and was watching TV. She glanced at the clock on the nightstand. Nine o'clock. Leah was too wired to sleep anyway. "Are you okay to drive?"

"I think so. Yeah."

"We need to go back," Leah said, stating the obvious. "We should assume he knows what we're doing, and if we don't return, he might get more aggressive."

"You're right," Mig said. "Let's meet at my place. And Leah, I'm sorry. I'm really, really sorry I didn't believe you."

Chapter 32

Mig beat her home. Avoiding the Prestwich Tunnel again cost her an extra hour, but Leah didn't care. Just the idea of navigating the tunnel at night jangled her every nerve. The garage door opened as the Blazer turned into the driveaway. Mig had been waiting for them. He opened the driver's side door, pulled her out, and enveloped her in a bear hug.

"I'm so sorry," Mig said into her ear.

"It's a hard thing to believe," Leah said, too tired to say more.

She'd driven straight through from Laramie, and she was swaying on her feet.

"You okay?" Mig asked, staring down at her.

"I'm feeling a little woozy, to be honest."

Mig gave her another squeeze and then unbuckled a sleeping Harper from her car seat. She stirred but did not wake as Mig carried her into the family room, where he deposited her next to Sofia and Mason on a pile of blankets on the floor.

"I thought we should all sleep together in here, until we get this figured out," he whispered.

Leah nodded, tucked Chicken under the blanket next to Harper, and sat on her haunches, gazing at the sleeping faces of the three children unaware of the threat looming over them.

"What are we going to do?" she whispered.

Mig rubbed his eyes. "I have no idea. But we're home. Like that fucker wanted. We need to think this through, but first, we need some sleep."

Leah pulled out her phone and glanced at the screen. It was almost three o'clock. Less than three hours until sunrise. She tugged off her boots, crawled into the sleeping bag next to his, and immediately fell asleep.

The ordinariness of the morning's routine contrasted with the dread pressing down on her as she made breakfast for the children. All three kids wanted pancakes and bacon, and luckily, the refrigerator had everything she needed. Mason put up a bit of a fuss when the bacon touched his pancakes, and the two girls scolded him for being "so weird," but Leah ended the rough patch by announcing the twins had a day off from daycare, and they could all hang out together for the rest of the day.

Leah sat down and opened her laptop to check email. Glancing through the list in her inbox, she saw there was one from the private investigator who specialized in adoptions. She took a deep breath and opened the message. Leah read it slowly, then read it again. Her mother refused contact, but her father, who was divorced and hadn't had any other children, was eager to meet her.

Leah gazed into space with unfocused eyes. A few days ago, she didn't even know she was adopted, and now she had a chance to meet one of her birth parents. She felt a rush of excitement, then a thin finger of fear. What if he was a jerk? What if there was a horrible hereditary disease in his—her—family?

Excited voices pulled her back to reality.

"It's not so windy anymore!" Mason said, peering out of the patio doors.

Sofia glanced at Leah hopefully. "Can we play outside?"

Leah thought for a moment, insides shriveling. Inside. Outside. It didn't matter. If The Copper Man wanted to get at the children, he could. "That's fine. Just stay in the yard where I can see you."

She watched the children dash out of the room, Harper in the lead. Any joy at seeing her daughter play so happily with other children was tempered by a sense of foreboding. By the time Mig appeared in the kitchen, hair wet from a shower and in a fresh change of clothes, she could tell by the hard set of his jaw and the distress in his brown eyes, he felt as overwhelmed and confused as she did. He fell into a chair and stared out the window at the gray sky.

Leah swept the dirty dishes from the table, wiped away the crumbs, and set a plate in front of him. "What is it?"

"I don't get it," Mig said, fork raised. "He wanted us here, but why?"

She started a fresh pot of coffee and sat across from Mig, staring into her empty mug. "I've been asking myself the same thing all morning, but I haven't been able to figure it out."

Her father had worked for the mine, but other than reporting on it, she had no association with it. Mig worked for the New Prestwich Copper Mine but had nothing to do with the death of George Cunliffe's son. The way Cunliffe had stared at her when she encountered him all those years ago stuck with her. It was his intention to snatch *her,* she was sure of it. She'd escaped Cunliffe, and he'd taken her brother instead. That had to be a big part of why Cunliffe seemed to be targeting her. It was the only connection she could think of.

That wasn't quite right. Since her arrival in Tribulation Gulch, she'd witnessed four deaths. This time, Cunliffe killed adults, not children. One had been a photographer, but the other three worked for the mine. Was revenge still his motivation? If so, maybe *she* wasn't the key, but his latest victims were?

"Did Morgan, Rick, and Gabby know each other?' she asked. "I know Morgan had just started, but I'm wondering if there's any connection between them."

"Not really," Mig said, dragging a slice of bacon through a puddle of syrup. His eyes widened. "Actually, there is. I forgot. We were all in the same meeting. A cross-functional team on Morgan's first day. She was there, just in case the issue came up during the mine tour, or that meeting we went to in town. The one she was supposed to be at." He frowned, shaking his head slowly, as if trying to work something out.

"What is it?"

When he didn't answer, Leah got up and poured their coffees.

"Are you going to tell me?" she finally said. "What was that cross-functional team meeting about? I mean, we're desperate here, so don't hold anything back. Not now."

Mig polished off the last pancake, pushed his plate away, and sipped his coffee. "It was about the tailings dam. Gabby was hired to develop the plan to repair the dam. Rick was working on it too. They said the dam had developed some weak spots and showed us some recent photographs of erosion. But they both agreed it wasn't as bad as the outside experts were making it out to be."

Leah sipped her coffee. "You saw the photos? What did *you* think of the damage?"

Mig shrugged. "Any erosion in the dam makes me nervous, but I'm not an expert."

"What did Morgan say?"

"Morgan had a more immediate problem," Mig said with a grim laugh. "Someone in the company—we don't know who—sent the TV crew the photos of the erosion, and Randall what's-his-name said they were going to use it if we didn't give them an underground tour."

Leah nearly choked on her coffee. "You're kidding? They're so pro-mine, they probably wouldn't even have run it. They were just using it as leverage to get pictures underground."

"That's what Morgan thought, but she didn't want to take the chance, and neither did corporate."

Leah ran a hand through her hair. It was a tangled mess. She hadn't bothered with her usual routine that morning. "Okay. Just thinking aloud. That means all four people who died—were killed—had some connection to the tailings dam. George Cunliffe blamed bad shit from the mine for ruining his water supply and his land. My brother's body was found in the tailings pond below the Prestwich Trestle, and that's where Cunliffe killed himself. There's got to be some sort of connection."

Mig lifted his eyebrows. "But what about the photographer?"

"I don't know. Maybe he was in the wrong place at the wrong time? I watched the video Daniel shot before he fell." Leah palmed her face with a groan. "I should have had you watch it because it showed The Copper Man standing behind me. Then maybe you'd have believed me." She barked out a laugh. "I'm an idiot."

Mig reached across the table and grabbed her hand. "You're kidding?"

"I am not." She stared down at her hand in his. It felt nice.

The sounds of the children laughing outside drifted through an open window.

Mig got up and began pacing next to the table. "Morgan went to the tailings pond after the meeting. She wanted to see it for herself. Gabby and Rick showed her around."

Leah glanced over her shoulder, as if expecting to see The Copper Man lurking outside in the hall, listening to their conversation. For all she knew, he was. The idea was enough to make her dizzy. "That's got to be it, then."

"It's got to be," Mig said, sounding as tired as he looked.

Leah took a slug of coffee and stared out the French doors. Mason was carefully walking in a straight line, arms stretched to the sides. The girls stood on a bench, calling to him. They were either making him walk the plank, or a tightrope. She got to her feet.

"So, what's he trying to say? Why did he want us to come back here? Is he trying to get us to do something? I think we need to go look at the tailings pond for ourselves."

Mig nodded. "I can sneak you in, but we shouldn't take the kids."

They left after Mig's babysitter arrived, with strict instructions to keep the kids indoors. As if that would do any good against The Copper Man. But at least it made them feel better—like they had some small bit of control.

Chapter 33

A narrow dirt road cut into the side of a hill led to the tailings pond. It was much larger than Leah imagined. In fact, she'd had it all wrong in her head. The Prestwich Trestle, where George Cunliffe had jumped and ended his life, stretched over a small portion of the tailings pond, far from the enormous dam she was looking at now.

On the bone-jarring drive, Mig explained the old dam had been built across a valley to take advantage of the natural depression. The dam itself was mostly made from mine waste.

There had been talk of building a new tailings pond using modern, safer methods, but they'd run out of land. A new pond, and a new dam, would require buying out the homeowners who lived a half mile away. Since most of those families had lived there for generations, they weren't interested.

Mig stopped the truck in the middle of the road, and they got out. Another early summer storm threatened. Gray clouds gathered over the Dinky Minors. The wind gusted and whipped Leah's hair. Slipping an elastic from her wrist, she swept her hair into a ponytail to keep it out of her face.

The tailings were a reddish-orange sludge with streaks of green and bluish-gray.

Leah looked around. The area was bleak, the colors otherworldly and disturbing. "How do you guys monitor the dam?"

We send up the occasional drone to look for breaches. Wells monitor ground water for seepage. We're planning a pretty elaborate network system—"

"I'm sorry, what? You're just *now* planning a monitoring network?" she interrupted.

Mig threw up his hands. "I know. That's what I asked too when I started. But no. Digging the shaft went over budget, so dam monitoring got pushed back."

"Of course, it did." Leah gazed across the length of the dam. "What are we looking for?"

Mig raised binoculars to his eyes. Leah held her breath as she watched him scan the massive earthen dam. His swift intake of breath and the hardened line of his jaw told Leah he'd spotted something.

"That," he said, pointing and handing her the binoculars.

She was no engineer, but even she knew what she was looking at was bad. Where the dam met the valley wall at the far end, an area appeared to be washing away.

"That's the spot that Gabby showed us during the meeting. But it was just a tiny crack." Mig rubbed the side of his face. "There's no way it should have grown this much in just a few days. We've had those storms. Maybe it was the rain."

"Or The Copper Man," Leah said grimly.

"Jesus," Mig whispered. "You think he can do that?"

"You didn't see what he did to Liam's room. He's killed four people, and he walks out of walls. So yeah, I think he's capable of poking a hole in a dam owned by a mining company that's pissed him off."

Mig gave the barest of nods. "Do you think he wanted us to see this?"

"Hell if I know what that monster wants," she said bitterly. The wind was making her eyes water.

Mig continued staring at the far end of the dam. "Maybe something else is causing the crack, and he wanted to bring us out here so we could see it and do something about it."

Leah snorted. "Yeah. Because suddenly, The Copper Man is an environmentalist and is trying to prevent a catastrophe. You're cute, but I don't think so." She tipped her head up at the sky and squeezed her eyes shut. Her brain was exhausted. She was tired of trying to guess what The Copper Man was doing. "How bad is the crack?"

"Bad enough I'm going to get some people out here before it gets any worse," Mig said. "Bad enough I'm going to text corporate and give them a heads-up." He touched her arm, then turned toward the truck.

"I'll stay here 'til you're done." Leah didn't mind a few moments alone. It was the closest she'd ever been to the place where Liam's body had been found. The pond was even uglier than she'd imagined. George Cunliffe had slit Liam's throat with a hunting knife, then transported his body in the cab of his truck, covered with a tarp, like Liam had been roadkill. Cunliffe probably waited until after dark to dump the body.

Her eyes were watering, and not from the wind. It had been a long time since she'd shed a tear for her brother. Her brother through adoption and not blood, as it turned out. The brother she'd left behind.

Leah glanced over her shoulder. Mig was seated in the truck with the door open, a long leg hanging out, cell phone pressed against one ear. She could join him in the truck and get out of the wind, but she wanted to give him space to talk without seeming like she was trying to eavesdrop for a story.

Leah looked through the binoculars again. It took some time to adjust the lenses and get her bearings. Starting at the dam, she scanned the pond, then she stared at the triangle shapes of the trestle. The old bridge was in such bad shape, she wondered how long it could remain standing. She continued her survey of the dam, until she'd reached the problem area.

Leah gasped. That couldn't be right. The crack, the one she'd seen just minutes before, had widened.

Panic bubbling up, she spun around.

"The dam!" she cried.

Mig raced toward her and then past her, coming to an abrupt stop, hands raised to the sides of his head. "Oh shit!"

"How did that just happen?" she shouted over the wind.

"I don't know," he said, turning on his heel. "It doesn't make sense." He sprinted back toward the truck.

While Mig called for help, Leah turned back to the breach. A thin trickle of sludge began to run slowly down the face of the dam.

Her mouth tasted foul. Her restless eyes traveled back to the Prestwich Trestle. It took a few moments to register the movement among the triangles at the base of the bridge.

A shape was moving across. A familiar, hooded figure.

An icy tingle ran down the back of her neck. With trembling fingers, she looked through the binoculars.

Black holes that passed for eyes stared back at her. It was The Copper Man.

Chapter 34

This time, Mig believed her. He hadn't seen The Copper Man floating across the Prestwich Trestle, but he hadn't needed to because she saw it, and he trusted her.

"The Copper Man is out to destroy the dam," Leah said. She described the documentary she'd watched. In life, he'd wanted to avenge his son's death, which he blamed on the mine. In death, whatever monstrous thing he'd become, perhaps he'd set his sights higher. Tribulation Gulch. When the mine reopened, it awakened his old rage. The town allowed the mine to open, and now it was going to pay.

Or something like that. Who knew how his dark mind worked. It sounded crazy, but no crazier than anything else that had happened.

They huddled in the truck, jounced by an increasing wind, and waited for crews to arrive to shore up the weak spot in the dam.

"I don't get it," Mig said. "The Copper Man didn't want us to leave. He wanted us back home. So now we're here, we saw what he's up to, and I've got people coming to fix it. So why risk that?" He groaned and smacked the steering wheel. "Oh shit. I hope he's not going to mess with my guys."

"Me too. Or maybe he just wanted us to come back and witness what he's doing. Like I did when he took Liam."

"I hope that's all. It's not like I can warn the guys to be careful. Like, careful of what? Watch out for the boogeyman? They're already spooked enough. One mention of The Copper Man, and we'll have another walkout."

"Can they patch up the leak?" Leah asked.

"Jesus, I hope so. Gabby was the expert. A couple of her people are coming over to take a look, so we'll see."

Mig checked in with the babysitter and learned the kids were fine. He went out into the wind and surveyed the dam, returning with the grim expression that these days seemed permanently etched into his handsome face. "I might be imagining things, but that crack seems to be getting even bigger. At this rate, that little leak is going to become a full-fledged breach."

"What's taking the crew so long?"

"It takes a while to get everybody together. Some guys aren't on shift, so they're calling people in. Then they've got to load the bulldozers and heavy equipment on trailers and drive them in. It just takes time."

He twisted in his seat and stared at the dirt road. Leah followed his gaze. A cloud of dust announced an approaching vehicle. Minutes later, a white truck roared up.

"They can't see you here," Mig said.

Leah climbed into the backseat and pulled a tarp over herself. The last thing Mig needed was the hassle of trying to explain why he'd brought an environmental reporter to check out the tailings dam.

The stiff tarp muffled the sound. Mig had left a window open a few inches, but between the wind and the plastic, Leah couldn't make out any words. The alarm in their voices was clear enough. Finally, the voices stopped, and Mig got back into the truck.

"They took some pictures and headed back," he said.

Leah threw off the tarp and clambered into the front, hair falling over her face. As she settled into her seat, Mig reached over and gently pushed a lock of her hair from her eyes.

"They think it's bad."

Her heart sank. "How bad?"

"Bad enough, but it's complicated. The engineers don't agree on the severity of the crack. One thought it's not good but could be fixed, no problem, and the other thinks it's bad enough the whole thing might go. He wants to follow protocol and send out an evacuation warning, but the other guy says it's way too soon, and it would cause unnecessary panic, so they're going back to hash it out on a call with corporate."

"What do you think?"

"I'm not a tailings engineer, but I'm worried. Especially knowing what we know about The Copper Man."

Leah took a deep breath to calm her rising panic. "If the dam breaches, how long before it reaches the neighborhood?" She was thinking of the development nestled in the Dinky Minors, along the banks of Prestwich Creek.

Mig frowned, pressing a finger into the fold between his eyebrows. "An hour and a half, maybe. It's hard to say. The rain we've had might make it move faster. Don't know."

Leah shifted, her knee jamming into the glove box. She winced. Staring straight ahead at the distant ridge of pine trees, she said, "We need to do something."

Mig turned to stare at her. She could feel his eyes boring into the side of her face.

"Like what?" He sounded wary.

Leah wanted to scream. Grab him and give him a good, hard shake. Instead, she took a deep breath and rolled her eyes. "Warn people."

"We can't do that," Mig protested. "The company's got a plan in place, and until someone pulls the trigger, I'm stuck here."

Mig needed to wait, but Leah didn't work for the mine. She could do whatever the hell she wanted, and she didn't need to involve Mig. In fact, it was better he didn't know. Plausible deniability, and all that.

She gave his arm a reassuring pat, which was as good as a lie. "You might as well take me home. I can't stay under that tarp for as long as you're going to need to be out here."

Chapter 35

After Mig dropped her off, she checked in with Patricia, who was still ailing, but at least her condition hadn't worsened. Leah went downstairs and arranged for the babysitter, Susan, to stay with the kids until she returned from "an unexpected work assignment," got in the Blazer, and sped off toward the Dinky Minors and the neighborhood along the creek below the dam. The rain had stopped, but ferocious winds buffeted the Blazer. Leah gripped the steering wheel a little tighter.

Before the neighborhoods around downtown Tribulation Gulch sprung up, Dinky Estates, as it was jokingly called by the locals, was where the early mine company officials had built their homes. She slowed down, looking around, noting the signs of prosperity. Expensive new SUVs in the driveways. Fancy outdoor furniture on deep-set porches. Attractive landscaping.

Mig had mentioned some of the new mine company executives bought houses at Dinky Estates. It was the one neighborhood that didn't involve a drive through Prestwich Tunnel. The houses were good-sized, but by Wyoming standards, they were not excessively large. However, the properties had something else going for them. They were charming. Worthy of a magazine cover. There was no town center to speak of, just a tiny market and a small park with a gazebo in the middle, which was deserted. No surprise, considering the weather.

Prestwich Creek ran straight through the middle of the neighborhood, which was why her parents decided not to buy there. For them, the convenience of a shorter commute to the mine was overshadowed by the risk of flooding. Leah suspected they never thought about what would happen if the dam breached.

She pulled up next to the park and turned off the Blazer. Leah had chosen the least conspicuous place to hang out for a few minutes and get her thoughts together. It was going to be tricky to explain why she was there, providing anyone was even home to hear her out. She knew she was going to sound like a crazy person, but she couldn't stay home and twiddle her fingers, waiting for the company to do the right thing. The residents deserved fair warning, because if her suspicions were correct, The Copper Man wouldn't be happy until he'd destroyed the dam and everything along its path, including Dinky Estates and Tribulation Gulch.

Leah closed her eyes and inhaled deeply. What she was about to do was going to make Mig very unhappy, and The Copper Man might shoot her down with a hail of copper nuggets if he figured out her plan. She hoped he was too busy directing his dark powers at the dam to bother with little ol' Leah Shaw.

Retrieving a fleece-lined rain jacket from the back of the Blazer, she set out for the house across the street, shoulders hunched against the wind. No one answered. There was no one home at the next three houses she tried. She scurried around the corner.

The man who opened the door looked to be in his seventies. He had a round, friendly face stuck on a skinny neck.

"I don't want any," he said without preamble.

Leah pushed her hood back so she could hear him better.

"Whatever you're selling, I don't want any," he said, louder this time, a spotted hand gripping the screen door. "Especially if it's religion. I told that Mormon fellow to take me off the list." He held up a hand. "I don't have a beef with the LDS. I feel the same way about Jehovah's Witnesses and the Catholics too." He reached around and tapped an engraved sign on the wall. It read: NO SOLICITORS. "You should have read that before you bothered knocking at my door."

Before she could explain, he was leaning forward and staring at her face.

"Looks like you got beat up some. You're not in some kind of distress, are you?"

Leah nearly burst out in hysterical laughter at the irony. Instead, she swallowed and said, "I'm fine, thank you." She hesitated. Now that she had someone's attention, her mission seemed impossibly daunting. "I'm a reporter. An environmental reporter. I got a tip from a confidential source that there's something wrong with the tailings dam at the mine, but they weren't ready to warn people. So, I thought someone should, so I'm out here."

The man blinked. "I worked at the mine."

To keep the conversation going, she said, "What did you do there?"

"I worked in accounting." He glanced over his shoulder, and when he turned to face her again, she could see in his eyes he was worried. "My wife is sick. Cancer. Are you sure about this?" He looked over her shoulder and into the street, as if expecting to see a hidden camera.

"I'm a little too old to be playing pranks," she said firmly. A gust of wind pushed on her back, and she swayed on her feet.

The man shivered. "It seems a bit far-fetched to me, you showing up here. I don't even know your name."

She had hoped to avoid it, but there was no other choice. Leah dug into her pocket, pulled out her Colorado press pass, and held it out for his inspection. It had her name and photo on it. The man leaned in closer, studied it for a moment, and nodded.

"Nice to meet you, Leah. I'm Doug. It's going to take you a long time to tell everyone."

Leah just had the same thought. For every person she met, she'd have to go through the same thing, hoping they'd believe her if they didn't slam the door in her face. Time and circumstances, were not on her side.

He continued. "Lots of people aren't home at this hour. They're at work or picking up the kids from school in town. We've got some snowbirds, too, and they're not back yet from Florida, or wherever they go. All the same, if the dam is going to go, we need to get to the store."

"The store?" she repeated. Was the guy loopy? Did he think he needed to stock up on canned goods, as if they were facing a power outage?

He waved a hand at her. The screen door shut in her face. Leah could hear him fumbling around just inside and wondered if she should bother waiting. She was about to leave, when he joined her on the porch wearing a jacket.

Doug shook a set of keys and said, "Let's go." He moved with surprising speed for a man of his age.

"Are there people at the store?" she asked.

Curtains parted in the front window of a house. A woman stared out at them and raised a hand in greeting. Doug waved a hand over his head and walked faster. Leah noticed he was limping.

The store wasn't far, just around the block. It was old. White-painted wood with a steeple.

"It used to be the old schoolhouse." Doug pushed the key in the lock. "We closed at noon today," he explained, switching on the lights. The store was small but well-stocked.

Leah was beginning to feel a bit like Alice in Wonderland, where nothing made sense. It was a relief to get out of the wind. It rattled the windows as if trying to get in. She watched Doug cross the room and throw open a skinny door. He pointed to a ladder inside.

"There's a bell up there. I was hoping you could give it a couple of rings for me. I'd do it myself, but this weather is doing a number on my knees." When he noticed the baffled look on her face, he said, "I should have explained. We use the bell for emergencies. It brings out everyone who's home to the park. It's an old-fashioned way of doing things, but we've done it this way as long as I can remember." He stared unblinking into Leah's eyes. "The thing is, you'd better have your facts straight. Because it will be the end of both our reputations if you don't."

Leah scurried up the ladder, sneezing in the musty confines of the vertical passage. Halfway up, she reached a small landing and spotted the dangling rope. She grabbed it with both hands and yanked it. The iron groaned a few times before the clapper struck. The bell rang, and so did her ears. When Doug yelled at her to stop, she wiped her hands on her jeans, climbed down, and joined him in the store.

Five minutes later, as they stood huddled in the park, the first residents ran down the street toward them.

Doug introduced her but did all the speaking to the astonished crowd of several dozen people. A few people had questions, but none seemed to doubt the legitimacy of her story. The big issue seemed to be timing. When would the dam breach? When did they have to be out? When would they be able to return?

"I'd get going right away, if I were you," Doug said. "That's what I plan on doing."

The crowd didn't disperse immediately. There was some discussion of where to go. A few decided to drive to relatives in Dubois or Jackson Hole. Others announced they'd head into town and wait it out there. If the dam failed, Tribulation Creek, and therefore the town, would be screwed, but it wouldn't be inundated with toxic sludge.

After helping Doug pack up a few things for his wife, who was recovering from a chemotherapy treatment, Leah helped the frail woman to their Yukon. She waved as she watched them drive off. Back in the Blazer, Leah started the engine and ran the heater for a few minutes, leaning her forehead against the steering wheel. She barked out a laugh of disbelief, and then tears stung her eyes, and she was crying. Of all the houses to pick, she'd lucked out choosing Doug's. She didn't even know his last name. He'd believed her, without too much fuss, and activated an emergency response that was as quaint as the town itself. No matter what the mine decided, at least the people living in the shadow of the dam had been given fair warning.

She called Mig, desperate to know what was going on, but he didn't answer. He didn't respond to her texts either. Not surprising. The crews had probably arrived, and he was busy. But she wouldn't be able to shake the worry. The Copper Man was out there. She had to know what was happening.

Leah called the babysitter, who picked up immediately.

"I'm just about to give them their dinner," Susan said.

Leah could hear the children laughing in the background. At least she had that to be grateful for—the kids were safe at home, unaware of the disaster their parents were trying to avoid.

"I really hate to ask this, Susan—"

Susan interrupted. "They're fine with me, Leah. Take as long as you need. I'm in no hurry to get home."

After she'd thanked Susan profusely, they hung up. Leah made a U-turn, following the line of cars out of the Dinky Estates neighborhood, then sped off toward the mine.

Chapter 36

It was a bad combination: Leah's frayed nerves, the wind, and the bouncy ride down the dirt road. Leah's stomach lurched with every bump she hit. Her unease worsened the closer she got. She'd forgotten about the security gate and didn't have a plan for getting past it. There were only two choices. Call Mig again and hope he'd pick up, or park the Blazer and walk in, which wouldn't be fun, given the distance and the weather.

As she rounded a bend in the road, she saw she needn't have worried. The arm of the security gate was open, and there was no one around to stop her. She stepped on the gas.

The wind was howling over the Dinky Minors. The Blazer rocked. It was just after five o'clock, but with the sun hidden behind a ceiling of clouds, it was impossible to tell the time of day.

It would be another quarter mile, she guessed, before the tailings pond emerged on her left. To her right stretched flat land covered in brush and rocks, and beyond it, a steep upward slope forming the foothills of the Dinky Minors. Pine trees covered the hills. The contrast between the two sides was stark: to the left a bleak, barren landscape created by man; and on the right, rugged natural beauty untarnished by the mine.

At the periphery of her vision, a movement on the hill made her jerk the steering wheel a little. Leah slowed to get a better look. There was something up there.

A shadow between the pine trees, moving quickly along the incline through the heavy vegetation. Another shape appeared beyond the shadow, this one solid. An animal. An antelope, maybe, or a mule deer. The shadow stopped.

Heart hammering in her chest, Leah slammed on the brakes, just in time to see the animal rise into the air.

Before her mind could process it, the animal was airborne, hurtling toward the Blazer in a high arc, twisting in the air as if carried by a tornado. Leah managed to duck behind the dashboard before the Blazer shuddered from the impact.

Breathing through gritted teeth, she raised her head and peered out the window. By some miracle, the windshield was intact. The animal—a mule deer—had landed hard on the hood. Leah looked around wildly for the thing trying to kill her—The Copper Man. But she saw nothing.

Unwilling to risk another encounter, she waited. After a few minutes, she remembered. If The Copper Man wanted to see her, there was nothing to stop him from perching on the passenger seat.

Leah stepped outside and surveyed the damage. There was no need to turn off the engine. It had stopped on impact. The hood had collapsed under the weight of the deer. The Blazer was a bloody wreck. Even if she could push the animal off the hood, she doubted the vehicle would run again. Leah tried it anyway.

A terrible noise came from under the hood, but that was all.

She called Mig, but it went straight to voicemail. Her only option was to walk the rest of the way to the dam.

Fastening the hood under her chin, she set out. After a few yards, the wind whistling through the brush, she began to jog, then run. She had no wish to be out on the empty road alone.

If she'd worn her sneakers instead of her boots, she'd be able to run faster, and she wouldn't feel the blisters forming on her heels. Through the wind, she heard the distant rumble of heavy equipment and the occasional loud beeps of a vehicle backing up. A few minutes later, she saw a cluster of white trucks and then a group of people in hardhats.

Heads swiveled. Mig stepped out of the group. He said something over his shoulder and then sprinted toward her.

"What are you doing here?" Before she could answer, his head tilted, and his eyebrows lowered. "We just heard people at the Dinky Estates are evacuating." His eyes bulged. "Was that *you*?"

Leah shrugged. "Maybe."

He shook his head. "Jesus, Leah. Are the kids okay? Why are you walking?"

The adrenaline was draining from her body, and she began to tremble all over. Shivers, like she was coming down with something. "The kids are fine. My Blazer's not." Her voice sounded far away, hollow, to her own ears.

What she really wanted to do, more than anything, was throw her arms around his neck and cry. But she didn't think he'd appreciate that with his work buddies around. It was bad enough she'd showed up.

"A deer hit my car," she said. Technically, that was the truth. Her chattering teeth and her fuzzy head made it too difficult to explain, and with the way Mig kept glancing over his shoulders at the group of hardhats behind him, she knew he needed to get back to work.

His frown deepened. "Jesus, Leah." He paused and rubbed her arm. "Are you sure that's all?"

She shouldn't have come. After alerting the Dinky Estates, she should have gone home, relieved the babysitter, and gathered the children around her for some nice, safe cozy time. Instead, she'd given into her insatiable need to know things that were out of her control, and it had nearly gotten her killed.

Instead of answering, she said, "What's going on?"

"A lot," he said grimly. "Scrambling to shore up the problem area, mostly. It's too much and too complicated to explain." Mig shoved a hand in a pocket and pulled out the keys. "Why don't you wait in the truck until I can take a break and get you home. If anybody asks what you're doing here, just say you're my girlfriend, and you were dropping off my dinner and hoping to give me a blowjob, but you hit a deer."

Leah snorted. "Your imaginary girlfriend sounds amazing."

Mig grabbed her arm and pulled her toward the truck. "I like my real one better."

She climbed into Mig's truck as the wind caused it to rock. For the next hour, she remained tense, on the lookout for The Copper Man. The area was busy, crews coming and going. With the steady drone of machinery in the background, her eyelids grew heavy and fluttered closed.

Leah woke with a start.

Mouth like sandpaper, heart bumping, she snatched up her cell phone. Three minutes past seven. In the dusk, portable lights illuminated the stretch of hardpack between the truck and the edge of the bluff above the tailings dam. The rumble of bulldozers and distant, urgent voices were clearer than before. The wind had died down.

Stiff and disoriented, Leah slid out of the truck. The wind had died down to a steady but tolerable breeze. Mig stood at the edge of the bluff, alone, surveying the dam repairs. She walked toward him slowly, fuzzy-headed from her nap. He didn't turn, but his arm went around her waist, and he pulled her close.

"Have you seen him?" Leah asked.

"No." A long silence followed. "Have you?

She sighed. "Yeah. The fucker threw a deer at my car."

Mig's hand spasmed at her waist. "You should have told me."

"You were busy." She watched a bulldozer dump a pile of rocks downstream of the dam.

They stood like that for five minutes, caught in a strange silence of mutual understanding and worry. Giving voice to their fears might make them real, so, they said nothing. And watched.

In the distance, a man screamed. The kind of scream that signaled surprise and fear, rather than pain. It was too far to see what was going on, but she didn't need to. Leah felt The Copper Man's presence.

Men were shouting now. Pandemonium had broken out among the workers.

Mig ran down the dirt road that paralleled the tailings pond. Breath heaving with panic, Leah pounded after him. They were halfway there, when her ears began ringing. A moment of dizziness made her stop. Her head felt heavy. Ahead, Mig stopped too and spun around to stare at her. He was standing next to a light stand, and Leah could see his expression clearly. He looked confused and surprised.

The ground was moving. Mig lurched toward her, arms outstretched for balance, as the earth shook. The violent tremor seemed to go on forever, lights swaying as Mig and Leah held each other. And then, as suddenly as the earthquake started, it stopped.

Down at the dam, the yelling resumed.

"Oh my God." Mig sounded dazed.

Leah's tongue was thick in her mouth. "That was a big one."

Together, they raced down the road toward the commotion. The work lights, buttressed by sandbags, had managed to stay upright and provided enough illumination for them to clearly see the chaos below. A bulldozer had fallen from the top of the dam into the tailings pond. Further down, below the dam, a second bulldozer was on its side. Several workers gathered around a man lying on the ground.

As Mig and Leah approached the group, one man turned to stare at the dam, eyes bulging. "It's going!" he yelled.

Hand pressed against her mouth, stomach knotting, Leah watched a chunk of the dam wall crumble. The trickle of poisonous sludge became a river pouring through the gap, widening the gash.

More of the dam collapsed as the breach grew.

Mig's shoulders slumped. Arms hanging loosely at his sides, he said, "There's no stopping it now."

Chapter 37

They never made it to Tribulation River with the kids, and now they never would.

The toxic sludge inundated Prestwich Creek, decimated the Dinky Estates, and flowed into the Tribulation River. The earthquake and breach killed four of the men working to shore up the dam. Three other people were killed as the mudflow trapped them inside their cars. And there was no way to know how many more would develop diseases because of their exposure to the deadly waste.

In the five days since the catastrophe, Leah had worked nonstop, producing stories for the website and the cable channel. She received and accepted a job offer to join the cable network as their environmental reporter. Her latest story referred to the collapse of the dam as the worst environmental mining disaster in Wyoming's history. The official cause was a six-point-two earthquake, but the locals blamed the company.

Not one of her stories mentioned The Copper Man, though she was convinced the monster had triggered the earthquake. Mig wasn't so sure. He thought it might be a crazy case of coincidence. Leah thought that seemed highly unlikely.

Some of the workers swore they'd seen a ghost hovering above the dam just before the earthquake. The college kid from Laramie interviewed a few of them and included the soundbites in a series of videos that, of course, went viral.

There were as many stories online about The Copper Man sightings at the dam as there were about the breach itself.

Since the dam collapsed, Leah and Mig had both remained alert, expecting The Copper Man's reappearance. Four days of hypervigilance, on top of work and the kids, had left them exhausted. On the fifth day, they dared to hope they'd seen the last of him.

As they walked toward The Greek Coffee Shop, holding hands, the kids running ahead of them to greet Patricia and Shelley, Leah said, "He was looking for revenge, and he got it. Maybe he's done. Gone back to hell, or wherever he came from."

"God, I hope so," Mig said, but he seemed uncertain.

Leah's chest went tight at the thought of The Copper Man continuing to torment them. They'd been through enough.

She stopped just outside the restaurant door. It was a beautiful, warm evening, the street bathed in the glow of a stunning Wyoming sunset. "So, do you think he caused the earthquake?"

Mig sighed. He'd done a lot of sighing since the dam failed. "Maybe. I don't know. Probably." He reached and gently tugged a lock of her hair. "Did you tell your mom about your birth parents?"

Leah nodded. "Yeah. She's feeling too beat up about the dam collapse to say I told you so about my birth mother. But she's being surprisingly cool about my father."

"Are you disappointed? About your birth mom?"

"I've been too busy to process it," Leah said as they went inside.

The café was full. Leah waved at Crystal. The satellite truck operator was at the counter, comparing tattoos with Zoe.

Patricia was sitting in a large, corner booth with the same dazed expression she'd worn since learning of the dam failure. But, ever the doting Gimme, she'd brought new coloring books and crayons and was handing them out to the kids.

It was the first time since the dam failed they'd been together for a meal. Patricia had not been her usual brisk self since she'd heard the devastating news. Venturing to the market after the disaster, she had gotten an earful from several angry residents for supporting the mine.

Leah noticed her mother twitch every time someone walked by or looked in their direction. Mig noticed too, and said, "You okay over there, Mom?" which nearly made Leah spit out her wine.

Harper looked up with disapproving brown eyes. "She's not your mom."

Mig chuckled. "Not yet."

Leah kicked Mig under the table.

Last night, they'd slept together for the first time. He'd proposed, and at first, she thought he was joking. But he wasn't. Even if the sex hadn't been amazing, she might have said yes right then, if it didn't seem so ridiculously soon. Instead, she'd asked to think about it. She was distracted by The Copper Man, worried he'd show up again, and she didn't want to make such a big decision in that state of mind. Mig agreed, but over the course of the last twenty-four hours, he had asked if she'd made up her mind at least three times.

Shelley looked up from helping Harper color in a fairy. "Uh oh, Colt Carter's coming over here."

Leah watched her mother cringe, which was very unlike her.

The owner of Hook 'Em looked tired. Colt had dark circles under his eyes, and it looked like he hadn't shaved in days. He nodded politely at Shelley, before scowling at Patricia.

"Hey, Colt," Leah said. Her voice held a note of warning. She hoped he wasn't about to make a scene.

"You've been doing a nice job covering the story," he said. Colt jerked his head in Mig's direction. "Can't be too comfortable for you. The mine's taking a beating."

Mig shrugged. "I'm a short-timer. I already gave my notice."

Leah turned to stare at him. "You did?"

"Yeah. It's pretty obvious what's coming. Between the lawsuits and the investigations, nobody thinks the mine will be operating for a long time, maybe years. That means big layoffs. But I have friends at The College of Mines down in Golden. They've been after me for a while to come join the staff as a lecturer, so I've decided to do that, and some consulting on the side."

Leah jabbed him in the ribs. Golden was just a few minutes from her house in Denver.

"We'll be neighbors," he said with a wink.

Leah glanced at her mother, but Patricia was too busy looking at Colt like he was a rattler about to strike.

Colt took off his baseball cap, rubbed a hand across his bald head, and turned toward Patricia. "With respect, ma'am, I think you should resign from the legislature."

Patricia paled.

When she didn't answer, Colt cleared his throat and continued. "Your unquestioning support of the mine has destroyed this town. The river's ruined, and so is my business." He gestured behind him at the street. "We're all screwed. The river was our lifeblood. Who's going to want to come now? Have you seen the river, Mrs. Shaw? The dead trout? It's heartbreaking."

Mig got to his feet and gave Colt a friendly pat on the back. "You might want to take it easy buddy." He nodded at Harper. "That's her grandmother you're talking about."

Leah could have kissed him.

Colt dipped his head, cheeks flushing. "I'm sorry, ma'am, but I needed to say it."

Patricia took a deep breath. "I understand, Colt. As much as it pains me to say it, I think you're right. I thought the mine would save this town, but it was the river all along that was the main attraction. I'm sorry I didn't see that. So, I'm retiring." She reached over and patted Leah's hand. "And I'll be moving to Denver to be closer to my daughter and granddaughter."

Leah gazed at her mother in astonishment. She didn't know what surprised her more—that her mother had just accepted responsibility for her role in the disaster, or that she'd finally agreed to move to Denver.

"I'm glad to hear that," Colt said stiffly, then left to join a group of people at the other end of the restaurant.

"Wow, Mom," Leah said.

Patricia raised a napkin and dabbed at her eyes. "Will you help me clear out the house?"

Leah nodded, thinking about Liam's room and the red sludge all over the walls and floor. Her mother hadn't mentioned it, so she must not have gone in.

"Of course, I'll help," Leah said.

"I can help too," Mig offered. "Whatever you need."

"There's something else," Patricia said, lowering her voice. "One of the things that kept me from moving was Liam. He's buried here. When I get too old to make the drive, promise me you'll bring me here once in a while so I can pay my respects."

A lump formed in Leah's throat. "Of course, I will."

"I'm an excellent driver," Mig put in, and they all laughed for the first time in days.

Chapter 38

Three months later

In the family room off the kitchen, Mig had the television news on with the volume turned up while he unpacked boxes. It was so loud, Leah could hear it upstairs in Harper and Sofia's room, which she was painting a sunny yellow. The kids were going through a phase, pretending they were triplets and trying to trick the new neighbors into believing it. The girls insisted on sharing a room, even though the house had four bedrooms. For now, they were using the fourth bedroom as a home office for Leah.

Leah and Mig had been married in a small civil ceremony. They bought a house in a suburb west of Denver, a short drive to Golden where Mig worked but still close to the news bureau in Denver where Leah filed her stories and did live shots. Her mother hadn't been able to sell the house in Tribulation Gulch, but Patricia had enough money saved to buy a condo in downtown Golden, next to Clear Creek trail. She cheerfully babysat all three kids when Leah had to work.

Leah peered out the window to check on the children playing in the backyard. Two other kids from the neighborhood had joined them, and so far, everyone seemed to be getting along fine.

She poured more paint into the tray.

"*A new order from the EPA outlines the steps the New Prestwich Mine Company must take following the breach of a tailings pond dam that devastated the town of Tribulation Gulch, Wyoming. Our reporter, Leah Shaw, has that story…*"

Leah dipped the roller in the tray.

Mig shouted from the family room. "Your story is coming on."

She sighed, placed the roller in the tray, and went downstairs.

Leah walked in just in time to catch her stand-up, which Crystal had shot on their latest trip to Tribulation Gulch. That assignment had caused endless anxiety. Leah refused to stay overnight in town and spent the entire trip looking over her shoulder, expecting to see The Copper Man. But there had been no sight of the monster, no animals or bodies landing on the satellite truck.

Mig pinched her butt and jerked his head at the enormous TV screen. "You look hot up there."

Leah pretended to scowl. She hadn't showered after her run, and she hadn't bothered to put on makeup. "And I don't now?"

Mig was moving in for a lecherous kiss, when the doorbell rang. He looked out the window. "We've got another one," he announced.

"Your turn," she said. Since they'd moved in three days before, a steady stream of neighbors on the cul-de-sac had stopped by to introduce themselves.

Glancing at the clock, Leah saw that it was close to five thirty. It was her turn to make dinner, so she ran upstairs, put away the painting supplies, and opened all the windows to air the room out. She opened the back door, told the neighbor children it was time for them to head home, and escorted them across the street.

Dinner was easy. It was just a matter of warming up what she'd made while the kids were at school. Her birth mother might not have wanted anything to do with her, but she was determined to embrace her Mexican heritage, so she was learning how to cook Mexican food and learning Spanish.

The tacos were a big hit with the kids. After dinner, Mig hauled Mason into one bath, while Leah herded the girls into another. It was hair washing night, which was an ordeal with Sofia. Leah had to hold a towel over her face the entire time because Sofia was afraid of getting soap in her eyes. The girls argued over which book Leah should read for story time, and in the end, Leah read a chapter from each and then tucked them in.

The bedroom was still full of boxes. Toys and clothes. Liam's old chest sat at the end of Harper's bed. Leah hadn't wanted to bring it, but Harper had insisted. While they were cleaning out her mother's house, Harper had discovered a box of photographs and sat a long time with Patricia, listening to the story behind each one. A framed picture of Liam in a cowboy hat sat on Harper's nightstand. She'd insisted on that too, even though it made Leah's heart twist in her chest every time she saw it.

Harper pouted as Leah kissed her forehead. "Don't turn off the lamp."

Her daughter's fear of the dark persisted, months after her encounter with The Copper Man.

"I won't," Leah promised.

"Not even after I go to sleep," Harper said.

"We have two nightlights in here," Leah reminded her. "And one in the hall."

"She still wants the lamp on," Sofia said. "I do too."

Leah kissed Sofia's warm cheek. "I love it when you two gang up on me. And I promise. I swear, I won't turn off the light. Goodnight, girls. I love you."

"And leave the door open," Harper called after her.

Mig was still in with Mason. He suffered from night terrors, and getting him to sleep on his own was a challenge.

Leah went downstairs, cleaned up the kitchen while drinking a glass of wine, then went back upstairs to shower and wash her hair. When she was done, she checked on the girls. Both were sleeping. Chicken had tumbled to the floor, so Leah crossed the room to pick it up. She tucked the doll next to Harper and was turning to leave, when something shiny on Harper's nightstand caught her eye.

It was a copper nugget.

Author's Note

If you're familiar with Wyoming, you'll know there is no such town as Tribulation Gulch. Since my in-laws live in the state, my husband and I have driven long stretches of the open highway, and I love those small towns with evocative names like Chugwater, Ten Sleep and Bar Nunn.

While Tribulation River, the Dinky Minor hills and the Prestwich Copper Mine are also fictional, the snow-covered Absaroka Range with its fault lines is real enough. It was important to locate my fictional town in an area that would yield both copper and a good-sized earthquake.

I developed an interest in copper mines when I learned my great grandfather and great uncles worked in the mine in Bisbee, Arizona. More recently, I discovered one of my grandfathers had come from Mexico to work in the copper mine in Morenci, Arizona, before moving to Los Angeles. It was hard, dangerous work. Then I read about new developments in the way copper is mined and suddenly, I couldn't stop thinking about haunted tunnels and all the things that could go wrong.

If you're wondering where a California girl learned about mutton busting, I saw several contests in Utah and Wyoming years ago when I lived and worked in Salt Lake City. Watching little kids hanging onto the backs of sheep stuck with me, and while I was writing the story, I knew Leah was the type of child who'd want to try something as crazy as that.

While I love my coastal hometown of Capitola, California, the beautiful and rugged terrain of the Rocky Mountain West will always hold a special place in my heart.

Thank you for coming along on this dark journey to Tribulation Gulch. With so many books to choose from, I appreciate you chose this one.

Debra Castaneda

About the Author

Debra Castaneda grew up in the San Gabriel Valley of Southern California. She wrote her first story in the fifth grade, a bloody murder mystery she handed in as an English assignment. After a career as a journalist in radio and TV, she now devotes her time to writing horror and dark fiction. Her novella, *The Monsters of Chavez Ravine*, is an International Latino Book Awards gold medal winner. She's an active member of the Horror Writers Association.

When she's not in her tiny office writing, you can find her taking long walks, making Mexican food, binge-watching creepy shows, and texting her two daughters. She lives with her husband in Capitola, California.

Subscribe to her newsletter for: bonus stories, the occasional giveaway, and the latest news at www.debracastaneda.com.

Stay in touch with her at: @castanedawrites on Facebook & @castanedawrites on Instagram

More Books by Debra Castaneda

Dark Earth Rising Novels

The Root Witch
Two strangers, miles apart, are connected by disturbing incidents in a remote forest. What happens on Halloween 1986 will forever changes their lives.

The Devil's Shallows
Eight miles of mystery. One night of terror. Residents trapped in a remote neighborhood confront the unimaginable.

Chavez Ravine Novels

The Monsters of Chavez Ravine
A 2021 International Latino Book Awards Gold Medal Winner! Before Dodger Stadium, dark forces terrorized Chavez Ravine.

The Night Lady
A rebel curandera, a plucky seamstress, and a young reporter are pulled into the investigation of a killer terrorizing Chavez Ravine.

Made in United States
North Haven, CT
08 June 2023

37507667R00174